Once upon a time, a long, long time ago, Paul Springer began entertaining children of all ages as an acrobat and clown. He played weird creatures in *Star Wars*, a weird vegetable in *Little Shop of Horrors* and a, well, weird performer on children's TV for TV-AM and Channel 4. He helped Roger Rabbit work with human actors in *Who Framed Roger Rabbit*? He even clowned his way through Shakespeare for the BBC. Now Paul writes, produces and acts. He makes programmes and films like *The Ink Thief*, and weird ones as well. He's currently doing another TV series and two feature films.

Paul lives and works with his wife, Joyce ('Miz Tiggle' in *The Ink Thief*). He is still a clown.

D1439639

THE
INK THIEF

Novelization from his screenplay

by

Paul Springer

Illustrated by A. Murti Schofield

A Piper Original
PAN MACMILLAN
CHILDREN'S BOOKS

First published 1994 by Pan Macmillan Children's Books
a division of Pan Macmillan Publishers Limited
Cavaye Place London SW10 9PG
and Basingstoke

Associated companies throughout the world

ISBN 0 330 33714 9

35798642

A CIP catalogue record for this book is available from
the British Library

Typeset by CentraCet Limited, Cambridge
Printed by Cox & Wyman Ltd

To Lesley Oakden,
for making it all possible

CHAPTER ONE

'Hello, Kiddies'

Sam Waverley was the sort of girl who knows how to enjoy an airport. In fact, Samantha knew how to enjoy most things. When the Waverleys came through the big glass doors into the Departures building, Sam was already surfing on a luggage trolley, her Walkman earphones full of rock 'n' roll.

Jim Waverley's idea of fun was his palmtop computer, and he was so deep into it that he didn't even see the airport. He didn't hear the jets taking off. He would have walked into a wall if Sam hadn't come zipping back just in time to steer him away from it and back to Alex and Joan, their mum and dad.

Jim saw his parents, all right. In fact, he glared at them. Alex and Joan smiled back. Jim was not amused.

'It's stupid,' he grumped, 'and I'm going to hate it. You're scientists. What do you want to go back to the Stone Age for?'

Alex put his arm around his son's shoulder.

'It's a beautiful place, Jim,' he said. 'You saw the pictures.'

'Yeah,' Jim snarled, 'I bet our new cave will have nice paintings of mammoths on the walls. It's primitive. How can I do my research without access to . . .'

Jim never got to finish the thought. His sister hit the family like a hurricane, hair and luggage trolley flying.

'I found the gate,' she stormed. 'You're not going to believe the plane, Jim. Wait 'til you see it. It's great! Come on!'

*

Big jets are big. Really big. They look like machines for jumping oceans with. The one in front of the Waverleys was properly big, shiny and modern. Jim and his parents walked toward it . . . and they stopped . . . and Alex and Joan looked confused, and looked at their tickets for Leaf Airways, and looked at the name on the big jet (which was Maiden, not Leaf) and . . . Sam grabbed everyone's arms and pointed and . . .

There, not far from the jet, was a plane labelled 'Leaf Airways'. Well, it was probably a plane. Once. It was rusty. It was weird. So was the pilot. Weird. Possibly also rusty. They knew this because he was waving to them from the cockpit. He wore a leather flying helmet with goggles, an old flying scarf, and a grin you could fry eggs on.

Alex and Joan Waverley looked at the plane, looked at each other, held tight to their children, and together the Waverleys started a journey into the world of the weird. And horrible. And wonderful. But mostly weird.

Inside the plane was no better than outside. Nothing was missing. It was all just . . . strange. There were seats to sit in: rocking chairs, armchairs, typing chairs. There was music playing. Cartoon music. Complete with bangs, boings and splats. In the chairs were the Waverleys, trying to sort out what they hoped were just strange seat belts. Alex and Joan looked around the plane and looked worried. Very. Jim looked like his mind was back on Mars, or wherever it went when he turned on his palmtop. Sam bounced with excitement and . . . a bell rang, and . . . a recorded announcement was played:

'Welcome to Leaf Airways flight 123456 to Leaf. Your seat has a safety cushion. In case of a bumpy flight, simply place this over your head until they go away. Your pilot will now attempt to take off. Should he succeed, we hope you will enjoy the flight.'

It probably won't surprise you by now to learn that Jim didn't even hear the announcement, that Sam got even more excited than she was, and that Alex and Joan looked very . . . worried . . . indeed.

*

Watch the plane as it wobbles down the runway. See the little bits falling off. Hear the terrible coughing from the engine. Now look inside. Everything shudders and shakes: the little curtains on the windows, the Waverleys, even the pleasant green-lettered sign on the wall saying: 'Don't Panic'. Perhaps you've heard of signs like this before from other books, or perhaps you're a galactic hitch-hiker and have actually seen such a sign. Well, this one is different. 'Don't Panic' isn't all it says. It can say something else too. Something the Waverleys will not be happy about. Fortunately it isn't saying the Other Thing. Not yet.

If you were outside the plane, you could see Sam's face glued to the window with a big grin and wide eyes. You'd have to be inside, though, to hear her yelling, 'Yes! Blast off!'

Three hours later things, and the Waverleys, were settled down in the little plane. Sam leaned across the aisle to Jim.

'Almost there,' she said. 'Landing in Leaf in ten minutes.'

Jim stared back at his sister. Then he stared some more. Finally, he spoke.

'Oh goody,' he chortled. 'Just us and the dinosaurs. What fun.'

The Waverley parents, Joan and Alex, looked like sensible, patient sort of people. Joan sounded like she was trying hard to stay sensible and patient as she said, 'Jim, that's enough. The Programme is paying us to go to a beautiful village and live a healthy life. Doesn't that sound pretty good?'

'No,' Jim grumbled. 'I don't see one good thing about it from a scientific point of view.'

Joan looked at her son, took a deep breath, looked at her husband . . . and Alex took over.

'Jim,' he said, 'we have been through this before. The balloon makers in Leaf have developed plastics and gases your mother and I never imagined. As far as the Solar Energy Programme is concerned, we have to work there for a while. Leaf is now on the scientific map.'

Map was possibly not the best word Alex could have chosen. Jim was on it in no time. 'The travel agents don't think it's on the map. It wasn't on any map they . . .'

With a scream of overstrained and rusty metal, the strange old plane suddenly dropped out of the sky like a stone. It twisted. It climbed. It fell again.

'Nyyow!' said Sam. 'Voom! Whoopie!'

No one managed to say another word as the family was gripped by G-forces. Streams of light whipped around them as though they were plunging through space at impossible speeds. The plane and the Waverleys were turned and twisted. Streaks of brilliant colours exploded like fireworks, and the fireworks began to giggle, and grow eyes, and stick out their tongues and zoom through the walls and zoom through the Waverleys and *now* the 'Don't Panic' sign changed and said the Other Thing. It said: 'Okay, panic!!!'

Then, suddenly, as abruptly as the lights and G-forces began, they stopped. The Waverleys looked around. They all seemed to be fine. It was very quiet. Then there was a voice: 'We have just landed in Leaf. Please stay in your seats until the airport has come to a full stop. Thank you.'

Birds were singing in the beautiful countryside as Sam and Jim emerged from a beautiful stone house into an equally beautiful morning. The village of Leaf looked fresh and new and hundreds of years old. In the kitchen window of their perfect new home, Alex and Joan waved. Sam waved back.

Jim didn't even notice all the waving. He was too busy arguing.

'You wouldn't know sense if you stepped in it,' he said.

'But it *doesn't* make sense,' said Sam. 'If Mum and Dad think what happened in that plane was a leak from the gases we were carrying, why didn't it get the pilot and . . .'

'Argonon is a very heavy gas,' Jim explained patiently. Well, patiently for Jim. 'Dad says a low pressure release would only disperse over a very limited area, allowing . . . oh, forget it. We flew into the Twilight Zone, okay?'

Sam looked at the lovely, sleepy village nestling before them. 'Well it's beautiful,' she said, 'whatever it is, and we've got the whole day to look around.'

Jim looked around. He considered. He spoke.

'It's great. Picturesque. Olde Worlde. Boring. I hate it.'

An old, ivy-covered gate opened onto a rough field. Screaming crows nested in a ruined gothic church. It looked spooky. It looked dangerous. Sam thought it was about the nicest place she'd ever seen. She made sure Jim was following her, and went through the gate. Jim was following. As usual, though, he wasn't actually paying attention to the world around him. He had the palmtop computer out. He was in a much more interesting world than the old-fashioned, crummy village of Leaf until . . . he walked into an old-fashioned, crummy stone wall. Well, a stone, anyway. Actually, now that he stopped to look around, it was a tombstone . . . in a lost-looking cemetery, in a dark wood . . . with no Sam in sight.

Puzzled, and a little edgy, Jim started to look for his sister. He didn't see her. He also didn't see the strange shapes forming in the shadows behind him. The shadows swirled. The shapes disappeared.

At the edge of the same wood, Sam stood in the sunshine. Her mouth hung open. Her eyes gleamed. She walked, then walked faster, then ran toward . . . a patch of deep shadow where twisted shrubs and trees almost completely hid a very old wooden building. There was a faded sign, hanging by one hinge. It was covered in cobwebs. She could just read the lettering on it: 'Jake Meadows – TOYS'. The shop window was boarded up. When Jim finally caught up with Sam she had pulled a rotten board aside, and was peeking in. She had her sketch book out, and was drawing a picture. Jim walked slowly and calmly toward her, as though he hadn't been feeling the least bit scared or lost.

Sam's pencil moved quickly. Her eyes were bright. The roof of the ruined shop had holes in it. Dusty light poured down through them onto . . . an ancient, cobwebbed display of antique toys. In the centre of the display was a big, once brightly painted wooden fish. Sam had started her drawing of the fish and was colouring it quickly as . . . Jim came up behind his sister and . . . Thunder crashed. Lightning flashed. Just for a moment Sam saw a pair of long, raggedly clothed arms with hands full of sharp claws rise up above the toy fish. The claws froze in the glare of the lightning, as though startled, then whipped back out of sight. Sam gasped, wheeled away from the window and gasped again as she smacked into . . . Jim, standing behind her.

'Did you see it?' Sam asked.

'See what?'

'The thing. The claws. It was alive.'

Jim looked at the old shop. He looked at his sister. He put on a creepy, TV announcer voice. 'She thought she was taking a walk in a sleepy village, but Samantha Waverley had just entered . . . The Twilight Zone . . . na na na na-na na na na-na na na na – teedlum! Come on, Sam, that cold front is going to produce a fairly violent electrical storm and' – a huge drop of rain splatted into Jim's face – 'we're gonna get soaked! Let's get home.'

Jim had to pull Sam into motion, as though bump-starting her engine. Even as they ran, though, she couldn't stop talking about what had just happened in the old toy-shop window.

'You should have seen it. *Big* arms, *big* claws. What's got arms like that? I could hardly believe my eyes.'

'I wouldn't,' said Jim.

'Wouldn't what?'

'Believe your eyes.'

Sam stopped dead. She glared at her brother. She was about to give him her best return shot when the skies really opened, and they ran for home. They never saw the eyes, which went with the arms and claws, watching them go.

It was already homey in the Waverleys' new cottage. Outside, distant thunder still rolled. There was an occasional flash of lightning. Here in the kitchen, though, it was all dry and safe. The room was full of boxes in various stages of unpacking as Alex and Joan set up the new family home. On a clear area of table, Sam finished adding colour to her painting of the toy fish. Jim, as usual, was buried in his computer.

'It's fine with me,' said Alex. 'You explore as much as you want.'

Dad's permission got a big smile from Sam, and a big, tired yawn from Jim.

'Just get a little sleep in between expeditions,' said Joan. 'Come on, you two. It's really late. Get to bed.'

Jim shut down his computer and eyed Sam's painting. Sam put her brushes in their jar. The family got together for their nightly family group hug. On their way off to bed,

Jim looked at Sam's painting, looked at Sam and whispered nastily . . . 'Welcome to the Twilight Zone.'

Sam managed to give him a warning kick, smile pleasantly back at her parents, and push him out the door ahead of her.

As they climbed the stairs to their bedrooms, Sam blew on her painting to dry a wet patch. Jim looked at his sister. He couldn't resist. 'You left out the Phantom of the Toy Shop. Where's' – Jim moved into his sister's face, playing monster – 'the claws?!'

'Very funny,' said Sam. 'Goodnight, computer-head.'

'Goodnight,' Jim sweetly replied . . . 'airhead.'

The moon was low in the sky. A cock crowed, and They came drifting through the Waverleys' garden. Strange laughter. Strange voices. Strange conversation: 'S'almost late.' 'S'pracally early.' 'Le's do it.' 'Le's hit 'em.' 'Le's thump 'em 'til they squeaks!'

Watch as the owners of the voices get to the front door. This isn't a movie. This is real life. Cartoons don't exist in real life, but . . . Thumper and Creaker look just exactly like cartoons. Thumper has a big padded bottom. Creaker has big clown feet. Watch as they shove their heads right through the closed door and into the Waverleys' hallway. Now their bodies follow their heads and . . . *ptoinnnngggg!* . . . they're inside Sam and Jim's house. They looked around, and . . . they *morph* into real people! At least they look real. They also look delighted. They look excited. They look at each other . . . then both rush to the stairs.

Creaker walks up slowly, his big feet making the steps creak. He listens carefully to the creaking sounds, testing pitch and volume. Thumper goes straight to the top of the stairs. He paces off a distance from the edge of the top step to far back on the landing. He licks his finger and holds it up, as though checking wind direction. He looks at Creaker. Creaker looks at him. Nothing happens. Then, as though on an invisible signal, Thumper runs across the landing, jumps from the top step, flies over the stairs and lands with a huge bass drum *thump* followed perfectly by Creaker's big feet doing two wonderful creaks on the stairs.

Creaker looks absolutely thrilled. He giggles with delight. Down below, Thumper is even happier with the result. Chortling merrily, the two of them turn back into cartoons as they slip out through the Waverleys' closed front door. Silence, and . . .

A light goes on and spills across the hall floor. As though running away from it, another cartoon of colours floats whimpering and gibbering across the hall, and up the stairs. As he goes he morphs from being a cartoon into a sort of cross between ET and a giant clown. He looks terrified. He looks around. He looks . . . *into Sam's bedroom.*

Come through Sam's door with Lorni Snoop. Yes, that's his name. Lorn and lone and snooping into everything, *all* the time. Watch him settle. He catches his breath. He looks around and . . . he mumbles and . . . he starts to snoop.

'Mmmm. Ooooh, looka. Na-haa. Oh. *Aaaaaaaagh!!!!!*'

Lorni has seen his own reflection in the mirror. Horrified all over again he tries to jump into Sam's wardrobe, only to find it occupied by a cartoonish family clearly ready to protect their night-time turf. They scream. Lorni screams. He shuts the door, runs to Sam's bed and tries to pull himself together again. Nice. Soft. Safe. He sits. He sighs. He feels . . . something . . . in . . . the . . . bed. It's Sam! Lorni screams in terror once more, leaps across the room and dives through the closed window without breaking it, turning back into cartoon colours as he goes.

There's a clatter of rubbish bins falling over. A cat yeowls. Sam stirs, then settles back into sleep. Silence, peace and . . . a flash of lightning crackles in Sam's window. There's a rumble of thunder and . . . a pair of raggedly clothed arms rise up over the sill. Two hands flick out two sets of nasty claws and wrap them around the window frame.

Watch as the head of a creature rises up over the window ledge and now, at last, we see who the horrible claws belong to. It's Toddy, a cat in the shape of a person (or a person in the shape of a cat). He looks rough and mean as he flickers through the closed window carrying a large sack. He stands and considers the room and Sam asleep in bed. His eyes glow in the dark. Finally he moves. He slides around the room, selecting treasures to steal and throwing them in his bag. He seems to choose the biggest, heaviest books. Shakespeare. A dictionary. An encyclopaedia.

Watch Sam. She stirs. She almost wakes. Toddy waits until she settles down, then . . . slowly he edges toward her bed. If this was a movie there would be nasty screeching noises on the sound track and you'd know that Sam was in danger, but here it is really happening and it doesn't take any sound effects to know that it's time to worry when you look at Toddy's widening eyes . . . his claws . . . his eyes . . . as he says '*Yes!!*' and the claws rise and *strike* . . . at Sam's painting of the toy fish.

Now Sam is watching too. She's awake at last. She sees Toddy put her drawing in his sack with much care and attention. She sees him turn like a cat and . . . walk straight into the wall and bump his head and stop . . . and concentrate . . . and then walk *through* the wall. Sam waits for a moment, her eyes as wide as those of the cat man with his prize fish drawing. Then, quietly, she slips out of bed, grabs her robe and shoes, sneaks out of the room, and . . .

A few minutes later Sam was back, dragging a sleepy and displeased Jim with her.

'Sam,' he mumbled sleepily, 'you had a dream. You are a very weird person. This room is a mess. No monsters. Just mess.'

Sam didn't listen. She went straight to the window, looked out, then pulled Jim over to see the view. There, on a roof, was the cat man, stretching against the early dawn sky.

'Well, Mr Rational?' Sam asked sweetly. 'Was I right or was I right? Arms? Claws?'

Now even Jim was excited. 'What a highly improbable epiphenomenon,' he said.

'Speak English,' said Sam.

'Sorry,' Jim said. 'English for the under-fives: I see it, but I don't believe it.'

'Well what do we *do* about it?' asked Sam, trying to keep an eye on where the strange creature might go next.

'Research, of course,' said Jim. 'We're scientists.'

'Watch that "we" stuff.'

'Well, I am. Don't you want to follow him?'

''Course I do.'

The two of them looked out the window again at the scene below, looked at each other . . . and charged out of Sam's room.

Playing cat and mouse with a nasty-looking cat man seemed to be Sam's idea of a good time. For once, what they were doing was also Jim's idea of fun. Looking into the mysterious, explaining the unexplainable, understanding life, the universe and weird things. They were quite enjoying themselves as they followed Toddy through the woodland graveyard, past the ruined, owl-hoot echoing, spooky church and turned a corner and . . . there was the boarded-up Toy Shop window. There too was Toddy, walking straight to the boards, concentrating, and walking straight *through* them.

'You see,' whispered Sam. 'Walks right through things, like I said.'

Jim had seen it for himself. Now he was thinking so hard you could almost see the smoke coming out of his ears. He pondered. He reflected. Finally, he spoke.

'Improbable, but not impossible. $E = MC^2$. You can get things from energy, and energy from things. Therefore . . .'

Sam could wait no longer. She grabbed hold of Jim and headed for the overgrown, mysterious Toy Shop.

'Come on, Professor,' she whispered as she dragged Jim forward.

'Oh, right,' said Jim. 'Let's go.'

Creep up to the Toy Shop and watch as Sam and Jim try the boarded-up window. They can't force it open but, close by, Sam finds a little wooden door in the undergrowth. For once, Jim is faster. Unhesitatingly, he dives in, with Sam right behind. Come with them. We're getting to the good bits. I mean the bad bits. Oh, frathersnaggits, you know what I mean.

Sam and Jim emerged from a dark chute into an almost equally dark, mysterious tunnel. There was a faint glow of light in the distance, and they headed for it. Cobwebs stuck to them. Things rustled and squeaked in the darkness. There was a distant sound of . . . an engine? Finally they came to a small pool of light, cast by a single candle. The candle was set on the skull of a dog. In front of it were two crossed bones.

'I think we should go home now,' Sam whispered.

'Not a chance,' said Jim, and moved off into the gloom.

Rather than let him out of her sight, Sam followed. The sound of machinery grew louder, and the light at the end of the tunnel grew brighter. They could see more. Ancient dolls and toys were nailed to the props and beams with old-fashioned pens going through them and into the wood. Other pens were jammed randomly into the walls, dripping long-dried ink.

The tunnel curved. The light from around the bend was brighter still. The sounds of heavy machinery echoed around the walls. Sam and Jim edged forward and found themselves looking through a perfectly ordinary wooden door into ... what looked like an abandoned, dusty, cobwebbed corridor in an ancient factory. It looked much too big to be under the little abandoned Toy Shop. There were doors and side corridors everywhere. The light and sound were coming from an open doorway right in front of them. They peeked into it carefully and ...

Come closer. Look over Sam and Jim's shoulders into ... a catacomb. A cavern. Underground. Big. Remember Frankenstein? If he shared a place with the Phantom of the Opera, it would probably look like this. The word we want for a place of this sort is probably 'gothic'. 'Dark', 'nasty', 'fabulous' and 'frightening' are also good words. There were the usual cobwebs. There was the usual smoke and clutter and weird devices. It looked like the lair of a vampire chemist with old-fashioned tastes in furniture. The walls were lined with shelf after shelf of glass containers, each filled with a liquid or specimen. Strange glass shapes bubbled and gave off oily smokes. A huge hour-glass dripped not sand, but ink. From a large dish some sort of organic slime was growing and flowing, like a slug's nightmare, into a container below.

This was all seriously weird, but there was weirder still. There was a big old desk, like a wooden, candle-splattered cathedral. It was covered with ancient books and documents, and well supplied with old pens, pen nibs and inks. No, that wasn't the weirder bit. What was weirder than anything else in the lair was what was seated at the desk . . . *the Ink Thief.* Weird? Well, he was weirdly thin and pale, weirdly frightening and yet somehow, at the same time, weirdly attractive. He had a certain . . . elegance as he turned the pages of a very large, quill-written, darkly confusing-looking and clearly very old book. Behind him, the back of the cavern was almost completely filled with a Victorian tangle of machinery and pipes. Amongst the pipes was Toddy, the cat man, hard at work. He pulled levers, turned handles, stoked steaming engines.

Sam and Jim's eyes were wide as they took in the scene and . . . suddenly Sam grabbed Jim and pointed. Toddy was tipping his sack out onto the Ink Thief's desk and . . . it was all Sam's books! Look how the Ink Thief studies them as Toddy stumbles back to his machinery. While he's outwardly calm, the Thief's hand is shaking slightly as he holds Sam's books. Without taking aim, he throws one in the general direction of Toddy and . . .

Toddy drops everything and makes a difficult catch look impossible. Clearly the Most Clumsy Cat In the Galaxy, he stumbles as he turns to the machine, wrestles with a stray pipe, and finally manages to drop the book into a big hopper. He handles handles, switches switches. A glow rises from the hopper and along a pipe. Toddy keeps an eye on its progress while he works the machines. The glowing area runs through the pipes to a spout across the chamber. Toddy drops everything again (this time on his toes), meowls, runs to pick up a small container and . . . makes it across the room just in time to catch a single drop of golden liquid as it drips from a spout. He looks at it and drools. Holding it carefully, he hurries to the Ink Thief's desk.

The Thief controls himself. He doesn't come forward. He waits for the golden drop to be brought to him. Still, as he reaches for it his hand is definitely shaking. Beads of ink stand out on his brow. He gulps the liquid down, sucking to get every molecule of it. He flicks the container away. Toddy catches it. The Thief studies another of Sam's books briefly, and tosses it to Toddy. And another. Toddy returns to the machinery, holding the books and trying to lick out the bottom of the liquid container.

At his desk, the Thief is mumbling to himself. 'Not nearly enough Power in books.' He consults the hour-glass, then looks at Toddy and raises his voice.

'It's all too slow! There has to be a faster way. I must have more Power, and I must have it soon!'

Edge in a little closer with Sam and Jim. You'll see and hear better. Stay with them, though, and stay near the door. Then watch . . . as the Thief grabs another book. He flings it hard across the room. Toddy is feeding the previous books carefully into the hopper, and working the machinery. The change of speed takes him by surprise. He drops the book he's holding, catches the new book, and moves faster. Another book flies in, and another. Toddy pauses. He looks at this one. It's Sam's sketch book. Sam sees it. So does Jim. Keep quiet. Keep calm. Hope that Sam and Jim do the same. Watch Toddy as he opens Sam's book to the drawing of the fish. He licks it, then looks at the Ink Thief. The Thief is not watching. He doesn't see Toddy as he waggles his hips and sticks out his tongue. Toddy might have got away with it if he hadn't waggled his mouth as well . . . but he did.

'Hmmm,' he said to the Ink Thief's back. 'Got my fish. Fooled you. Mm-mm-mm. *Bad* cat.'

The Thief wasn't sure what Toddy was talking about, but he knew he didn't like the tone. He started flinging one book after another at the cat man, walking ominously toward him all the while. Toddy grabbed the books, threw them into the hopper, and worked the handles and levers. He threw Sam's sketch book with the others, realized what he'd done, caught it just before it fell in and . . . the Ink Thief loomed over him. Toddy looked at the sketch book, looked at the Thief, looked at the sketch book, looked at the Thief, looked sad and frazzled and dismayed, and dropped the sketch book into the hopper. He picked up the remaining books, and was about to add them, when something incredible happened.

The hopper began to shake like an earthquake. It glowed. The glow and vibration transferred to the pipes. The walls shook. The Thief and Toddy watched in astonishment as Power built up to the bursting point. The Thief was puzzled. Excited, but puzzled.

'It was a child's drawing,' he said. 'It was kiddie blah. Kiddie blah? Massive power from wretched children? I wonder . . .'

As you watch with Sam and Jim you're edging too far out into the light. Stay near the door. You never know what might . . . The Thief is wandering this way. Ease back into the shadows. He hasn't seen. He's too busy thinking and watching the machinery losing its rivets. Toddy's busy too. He grabs his small liquid container and rushes to the outlet pipe. He looks at the Power building up, looks at the size of the container, and rushes away. In an instant he's back, with a big jar. He looks up the outlet. It's steaming. He looks at the jar, disappears again, and reappears with a great big bucket. Right. That's it. He's ready. Something clearly has to give, or the machinery will fall apart from the strain. Toddy holds the bucket under the Power outlet. Nothing. He looks up into it and . . .

A torrent of golden Power bangs him to the ground, knocking the bucket from his hand. He gets back to his feet. He gets the bucket in place just as the flood of Power ends. He only saves half a bucket. He offers this to the Ink Thief, expecting the worst for having lost most of it. The Thief, however, is not upset. In fact, he smiles as he says, calmly, 'Not to worry.' He lifts the bucket and drains its contents. His eyes shine. Every cell of his body fills with Power. Power crackles around him like yellow electricity as he says, happily, 'I suspect there may be more where that came from. What a fool I've been. Oh, silly, silly *moi*. There had to be a better way, but children? Perhaps they're special children.'

There's a mad light of inspiration in the Ink Thief's eye as he lifts Toddy up by the scruff of the neck. He walks the cat man toward the tunnel entrance where Sam and Jim are hiding, and as he walks he speaks. 'I must find out. Go back to that house in the village. Find those nasty, stupid, horrible, smelly children, and bring them to me.'

Sam and Jim saw the Thief coming straight toward them with Toddy. They turned. They ran. They stopped. Standing there, blocking their way, was . . . it couldn't have been a rat. Rat's don't come gorilla-sized . . . do they? It looked worn, and tough, and horrible. It wore black leather. It had nasty eyes and nasty teeth and big, nasty, ratty hands extended toward them as it leered: 'My name is Aloysius, an' I'm nasty an' I'm vicious. Go on, little kiddies, make my night.'

The Rat did a small lunge forward, and Sam and Jim took a small jump back . . . back to the approaching Thief. Behind them a giant Rat. In front of them the Thief, looking happy and saying, 'I want those children,' and suddenly seeing them and saying . . . 'Why look, they're here. Wonderful, isn't it, the way destiny serves me? Hello, kiddies . . . nice kiddies . . . Get them, Toddy!'

Looking at the situation from where Sam and Jim are standing, you can see there's no place to run. Then Toddy comes forward, claws out and . . . Sam runs between his legs. She grabs his tail, keeps running, and Toddy is flipped head over heels onto his back. He's up in an instant, though, and there's no way out. He plays cat and mouse with Sam and Jim. Aloysius the Rat is amused. The Ink Thief quivers with pleasure. His nostrils flare, and a dribble of ink escapes from between his black and sensitive lips. Aloysius coaches Toddy through the chase.

'Be a bad cat!' 'I'm a bad cat!' 'Really bad.' 'I'm really bad!' 'Now get 'em.' 'Yeah, I got 'em!' Toddy tears in and misses his final pounce completely as Sam puts some moves on him. Before he knows it she and Jim are down the tunnel. Toddy chases them. The Thief does a little nod to Aloysius, who starts toward the tunnel and . . . Toddy comes belting back into the Thief's lair, yeowling as though chased by a pack of wolves. He runs straight to the Thief and hides behind him and there, in the doorway of the lair

are . . . Sam and Jim. The Thief smiles, reaches out his awful hands invitingly and then . . . his smile freezes and cracks. His jaw muscles stiffen, his eyes narrow, and his expression reforms into a sneer.

There's someone behind Sam and Jim. Someone who stops the Ink Thief cold. What kind of hero, what Superman, what Indiana Jones could . . . hang on. Wait a minute. It's . . . a Librarian? A prim, grey-dressed, spectacle wearing, old-fashioned, Victorian librarian!?

The Thief has controlled himself. He smiles a cold hard smile as he says: 'Ah. Miz Tiggle. How very . . . very.'

Prim and bookish though she looked, Miz T approached the Thief with gunfighter confidence and a look that could cut through armour plating. Aloysius, seeing her head for the Thief, slipped quietly away. Sam watched this unlikely hero with approval, and edged forward to support her. The Thief's smile grew broader, more wicked. Toddy, sheltering behind him, growled at the approaching females. Sam growled back *and* pulled faces at him. Miz T, meanwhile, went right up to the Thief. This was nose to nose, eyeball to eyeball stuff.

'Right,' said Miz Tiggle. 'I've had enough.'

'I, on the other hand, have not,' said the Thief, '. . . but I will.'

'Now you listen to me, my boy,' said Miz T. 'Because I'm OOB Librarian, the OOB have let you play your silly games with Power. Boys grow out of these things, I said. Give him a few more centuries, I said, but I was wrong. You leave these children alone and start thieving properly, or—'

'Or face the wrath of the boobs in the OOB?' the Thief sneered.

'Stay away from the children. You've already been barred from the library. Don't make us . . .'

The Thief was suddenly not paying the slightest attention to Miz Tiggle. He was watching Jim. Jim, looking at the contents of the lair with total fascination, had just come to the big, dark book on the Ink Thief's desk.

Have a look. Go over to the other side of the desk and see Jim's eyes widening as he looks at the huge old book. He's practically bursting with excitement.

Watch Miz T and the Thief watching Jim, and the Thief saying: 'Not a lot you can do, is there . . . *Miz* Tiggle? The Book seems to have the boy.'

Now listen to what Miz T whispers to Sam: 'Samantha, go get your brother. It's very important that we get him away from here right this minute.'

Sam started to ask why, then saw the look on Miz Tiggle's face and went straight to Jim, wasting no time.

'Come on, motor-mind,' she said. 'We're getting out of here.'

It was as though Jim hadn't heard her. He was practically glowing with excitement, or something, as he said: 'It's a quantum chemistry, Sam, and infra-phenomenal physics. It's what science dreams about. Infinite power. Perpetual motion. People could have everything. No one would ever need to be hungry, or poor, or fight wars. We could save the environment and . . .'

It was Sam's turn not to listen. 'Jim,' she said, 'Miz Tiggle has just taken the trouble to save *us*. Now you can come quietly or I can drag you home. What's it gonna be?'

Suddenly, the Thief was with them at the desk. He

looked at Jim with interest, even friendliness. He pointed to the book. 'Do you like it, boy?' he asked.

'It's wonderful,' said Jim. 'Infinite power, and so easy.'

The Thief observed Jim with hugely increased interest. 'Easy?' he asked. He looked carefully at Jim as he said, 'Yes, it is wonderful. All the Power in the Universe, and all it takes to get it is . . .'

'Finding the right sources,' said Jim, 'for infra-physical, sub-phenomenal . . .'

Look at the anger on the Thief's face as Sam and Miz T interrupt his little conversation with Jim. Just as the smelly child was about to explain it all, the *females* had to get in the way. Before he knows it Sam has grabbed Jim, and the awful Tiggle is standing between him and the children, saying: 'Samantha and James will be going now, and they won't be back. The OOB will see to it that . . .'

The Thief has had enough. 'Oh, please. Spare me. That pathetic, bumbling, style-free bunch of imaginary idiots?' He turns his attention to Jim, being half-led, half-pulled by his sister toward the exit. Jim clearly doesn't want to leave. As he goes, he drinks in the lair and . . . the Thief calls to him.

'I'll be sorry not to see you again, young Jim. Together, we could have changed the world.'

Miz T is having none of this. 'The world is just fine as it is, thank you very much. Come, children.'

Miz T ushers Sam and Jim through the exit from the lair. The Thief practises his killer smile on their backs and Miz Tiggle stays between children and lair as they walk down the cobwebbed corridor. This puts Sam in the lead, and Miz T has to call out to her, 'Fifth door on the left, Samantha.'

Sam counts doors, opens the fifth and steps through into . . . the creepy tunnel. Follow her in. There, in front of you, is the cave with the dog skull, crossed bones and candle. Lounging against the skull is Aloysius. The sight of Sam brings him quickly to his feet, smilingly wickedly. He advances toward her, blocking the tunnel. Sam stands her ground.

'Out of my way, you stupid rat.'

'Dirty rat,' says a very angry Aloysius. 'Dirty rat. The line is "Out of my way you *dirty* rat", only you don't got what it takes ta . . . whoops! Evenin' Miz Tiggle.'

'Good night, Aloysius,' Miz T says as she appears behind Sam. The gigantic Aloysius is suddenly as meek as a baby ratlet.

'Scuse me,' he says. 'I gotta go see a cat about a canary.'

Aloysius was back into his monster rat hole as fast as he could move. Sam looked at Miz Tiggle with admiration.

'Sorry about that, Samantha,' said Miz T. 'I meant the fourth door. Never mind. This will do.'

'They're all afraid of you,' said Sam.

Miz Tiggle started Jim moving forward again as she replied: 'I'd rather think of it as respect. Come through here.'

Miz T opened a door in the stone, taking them back into the cobwebbed corridors. Jim paid even less attention to the world around him than usual. He kept looking back in the direction of the Ink Thief's lair. It took Miz T and his sister to keep him moving away from it.

'Who is he?' Sam asked Miz T.

'Who's who?'

'The horrible bald creep.'

'He's the Ink Thief,' Miz T said. 'The cat thing is his servant, Toddy.'

'Am I missing something', asked Sam, 'or is this all very strange? An old Toy Shop with a cat man and a rat man and a master who looks like a vampire. I mean, it's the end of the twentieth century. Imaginary stuff like that only happens in movies.'

'My goodness,' said Miz T, 'is that the time?'

'Sorry, what?'

'Late twentieth century?' Miz Tiggle seemed really surprised. 'I somehow thought it was earlier, or possibly later. Never mind. Here we are.'

Miz Tiggle opened a door. There, framed in the doorway, was the Waverleys' new cottage.

'How . . .?' asked Sam.

'It's something to do with dimensions,' Miz T explained (if you can call that an explanation).

'Now, take James home. Leaf is a wonderful place. Inspiring. Your family will do very well here. Just keep your brother out of the Toy Shop.'

Sam turned to Jim, and found him looking longingly back down the corridor, totally uninterested in going home. She took his arm gently and eased him through the doorway into the fresh night air. 'You heard the lady,' she said. 'Home, James.'

Jim looked around as though waking from a dream. Sam turned back to Miz Tiggle. 'Thanks, Miz T. You know, I wondered . . .' Sam's voice trailed off. Miz Tiggle had disappeared. So had the doorway they just walked through. There was nothing there but an old stone wall and the night. Sam looked at where the door wasn't, then at Jim. Jim was acting normally again (by his standards). He smiled at his sister's confusion.

'Infra-phenomenal physics,' he said.

'Looks like magic to me,' said Sam.

'That's just 'cause you don't understand it. Come on. It's starting to get light. Let's go home.'

'What do we tell Mum and Dad?'

'About what?'

'All of that. The Ink Thief. Miz Tiggle. The Cat. The Rat.'

'Never heard of 'em,' said Jim.

'Yeah, well wait 'til I tell 'em that . . . and . . . They wouldn't believe me, would they?'

'I wouldn't,' said Jim. 'Would you?'

Sam tried to think of a thousand good answers to this, couldn't come up with one, and took a deep breath of frustration. For once it was Jim who took *her* hand and pulled her home. The door was unlocked, as they'd left it.

Watch them as they go into the house in the early dawn light. Wind stirs the garden foliage. An upstairs light goes on. Something else stirs the foliage . . . a dark shape emerging from the shrubs and slinking up to the cottage. The upstairs light goes out again, and . . .

Look closely at the dark shape in the garden. It's Toddy. In his paw he holds a large envelope. He looks up at the recently darkened bedroom window, puts the envelope in his mouth, and flicks out his claws. Digging them into the masonry, he begins to climb the cottage wall. Distant lightning flickers, and there's a far off rumble of thunder.

CHAPTER TWO

Strange Books

Morning came to Jim's room, lighting the clutter of boxes, clothes, computers, books and mess with sunbeams. It was quiet until a blackbird sang outside the window. Then it was quiet again until . . . a fist thumped on the door. Quiet. Sam never liked quiet, and she certainly wasn't having any of it now

'Jim, come on!' she called from outside his door. 'You said right after breakfast, and breakfast was *years* ago. Dad's made sandwiches and we've got a whole 'nother day to look around.'

The room stayed quiet, and Sam knocked again, even louder. 'Jim! Okay. I was polite. I knocked. I waited. I'm counting to ten: 12345678910 right, that was me being patient. Now it's back to the sister you know and love. I'm comin' in and we're going' – Sam opened Jim's door. The room was still empty. Sunny, but empty. No Jim – 'out.' Sam finished her sentence looking puzzled and then . . . she saw the letter. It was on a parchment-coloured sheet of paper with scratchy, inky writing. Sam knew it was from the Ink Thief even before she picked it up and read:

Together we would have the Power to make a perfect world. The Book is yours. Come.

Sam's jaw set in a line Clint Eastwood would be proud of. She fumed. She wodged up the note, threw it at the wall, turned and ran out of the room.

*

It's a creepy, cobwebbed world inside the Toy Shop. In a corner, there's a big toy merry-go-round. Spiders move in the gloom, using the toys to build Web City. Dust sparkles in the sunlight from the broken roof. Something's moving in the display. Turn slowly . . . creep up quietly and watch as raggedy arms and claws reach for the toy fish at the centre of the display and . . . they freeze at the sound of a thump outside the window. The claws pull back and . . . Sam peeks through the boards and has a quick look around and . . .

Sam left the window and headed purposefully toward the side of the shop. Toddy watched her go. He watched her turn the corner and head for the little side door into the underground corridors. He giggled as he left the toy-shop window and went back downstairs.

Through the dusty cobwebs, Sam looked down the long corridor. Water dripped into a pool on the floor. A spider dangled momentarily in front of her, then dropped out of sight. Covered in cobwebs, Sam kept moving forward until . . . she realized that she was lost. There were doors and openings into other corridors everywhere, and no way to know where to go next. Sam paused.

Listen. Something's coming. There's a scrabbling. There's a mumbling. Hide with Sam and watch as . . . something shuffles out of a side corridor. It looks like a walking pile of rags, dust-cloths and mops pushing a trolley. It stops. It mumbles. It goes to the trolley, pulls out a big cobweb, and hangs it on a beam. Back at the trolley, it reaches into a bucket and comes up with a handful of slimey goo which it throws at the wall. Another handful goes on the floor. A

third gob heads straight for Sam. She ducks, it splats and runs down the wall next to her and when she straightens up . . . the bizarre thing is gone.

Come along as Sam edges back out into the corridor. She moves forward and a door ahead of her opens and . . . there is Aloysius the Rat. He looks her up and down and begins to laugh. It's the kind of nasty laugh that starts quietly at ground level and grows until the walls tremble. Surprisingly, Sam doesn't look particularly frightened. Still, she backs carefully away until she comes up against something. It's probably not a wall. Walls don't usually move. Sam turns. It's Toddy. As Sam edges away he smiles and waves a friendly set of claws.

So, in one direction a big cat. In the other an even bigger Rat. Does Sam panic? Does she run screaming? She does not. She squints at them. She pushes up her sleeves and raises her fists, and she says: 'Okay. Who's first?'

This is not what he expects a girlie to do when faced with a big monster type like himself, and Aloysius is momentarily confused. Toddy, of course, is permanently confused. Puzzled, they edge in on her. Sam stands there looking tough, draws the two of them close around her . . . then slips between Aloysius' legs and runs for it. The courageous attack Toddy has just launched winds up colliding with Aloysius. By the time Aloysius has finished using Toddy for a punching bag and realized what's happening, Sam is gone and . . .

We're moving fast, running with Sam down a side corridor . . . and an arm reaches out . . . and Sam is practically pulled off her feet in mid-run and through a doorway and . . . she's gone. There's nothing but cobwebs and the sound of dripping water.

*

Things were also dripping in the Ink Thief's lair. Bottles full of strange liquids spilled coloured drops into the candlelit gloom. A disgusting, bubbling, organic brown mass was half-frothing, half-climbing out of a jar into a bowl on the shelf below. Bats flapped into the semi-light, and disappeared again into darkness. The Power machine steamed quietly.

At the Ink Thief's desk, Jim and the Thief sat side by side in front of the huge Book. It was a strange combination: the dark, bald, ageless figure seated next to the young boy. They were studying the Book together, and talking excitedly and . . .

In another part of the universe, or Toy Shop, or whatever, Sam was also in a strange place with strange company. It looked a lot like . . . a library. What had just pulled Sam in from the corridor was harder to identify. It was shaggy, like a dog. It was barking . . . like a dog. It was acting like an over-excited puppy, but . . . it had a body like a person and it was using hands to pull Sam.

'Okay,' Sam laughed. 'I'm coming. What are you? Where are we?'

The creature cocked its head, panted for a moment and then . . . it talked. 'Library. Doggy Bump. 'Maginary mongrel, answers to da name of . . . Dog! Come. Good girl. Come!'

Running around her, jumping up on her and pulling, Dog guided Sam across the library. Shelves and stacks reached up to a balcony with yet more shelves going off into the impossible distance. Then there were the signs: 'QUIET IN THE LIBRARY' and 'SILENCE PLEASE'. Dust motes danced in shafts of coloured sunlight through the stained-glass windows. Dog backed through a door and pulled Sam behind her and there was Miz Tiggle, reading a book, and Dog kept on pulling and Miz Tiggle, without looking, put out her hand and . . . Dog backed right into it and stopped and Miz Tiggle looked at Sam and said:

'The OOB are upset, to put it mildly.'

'Well, I don't know who the OOB are,' said Sam, 'but they're not as upset as I am. That creep under the Toy Shop wrote a letter to my brother . . .'

'Exactly,' Miz Tiggle interrupted, 'and now your brother is big trouble.'

Sam was by now well confused. 'Well, what do we do?' she asked. 'Is Jim down there? Can you . . . what do you mean, my brother *is* big trouble? You mean he's *in* big trouble.'

'That too,' said Miz Tiggle.

As Sam spoke, Dog was right with her. She looked from Sam to Miz T, nodded yes and no to Sam's questions so hard that her head looked in danger of falling off, and generally tried to be helpful. She wasn't, but she certainly was trying.

'There's a happy ending,' Miz Tiggle commented, 'of course . . . sit! Not you. Dog. Then there are also some unhappy endings, and a few of them are really quite nasty.'

'How?' asked Sam, 'do I get the happy one?'

Miz Tiggle had to reflect on this. 'I'm not sure you did . . . I mean I'm not sure you do. There. You see . . . I told you they were worried.'

Miz Tiggle pointed, and Sam's gaze followed her gesture across the parlour to a tall bookcase full of ornate books. Washes of colour were drifting out of them, floating through the air and turning into shapes . . . cartoons . . . people (practically). There were Lorni Snoop, Thumper and Creaker, not to mention Shake Rattle and Roll.

'What *are* they?' Sam asked.

'Bumps,' Miz T explained.

'Uhhh-huh. And Bumps are . . .?'

'My dear girl,' said Miz T, 'don't you ever go to sleep at night?'

'Y-e-e-s. And . . .?'

'And Things Go Bump in the Night.'

'Right . . .' Sam allowed, cautiously.

'Well, these are them,' said Miz T. 'This is they. Frathers-naggits! You know what I mean.'

Sam didn't have the slightest idea what Miz T meant. 'But what *are* they?' she asked again.

'Imagination,' Miz T said. 'What the world is made of. What's in all the books. Also worried.'

Sam looked at the Bumps. They did look worried. Especially Lorni. 'R-R-Really worried,' he stuttered, 'c-c-'cause . . .'

The Bumps had an audience. Sam was listening to them. This was too much for Shake Rattle and Roll. They had to do what a Bump's gotta do, and they were the Boogie Bumps so they started to boogie . . . and sing:

> Your brother's back, and there's gonna be trouble
> One Thief's bad, but two of 'em's double
> Hey, na nee na, your brother's back!

Amazingly, Lorni finished the verse with a wonderful rock 'n' roll scream: 'Waaaaaaaaaaaoh!'

No one was more surprised by this than Lorni. He panicked at the sound of his own voice. He hid behind Sam. 'Somebody screamed! Somebody screamed!' he screamed.

Sam was not amused by any of this. 'Oh, puhleese!' she shouted. 'Can you people . . . things . . . Bumps . . . get serious for just a minute? My brother is trapped downstairs with that crazy person . . .'

'Bump,' said Miz T.

'What?'

'That crazy *Bump*. He's a Bump. He's a figment of his own imagination.'

'He's got a pretty horrible imagination,' said Sam.

'Well,' said Miz T, 'I wouldn't exactly say he's *horrible*.'

Perhaps Miz T wouldn't say it, but the Bumps would. They said, 'I would,' 'He's not good,' . . . and they were off and rockin' again:

> Let's rock . . .
> He's horrible . . .
> Rockin' . . .
> Horrible . . .
> Rockin' . . .
> Horrible . . .
> Unh! He's not good.

Lorni couldn't stand it any more. He had to sing:

> Oh, yes, yes, yes, that Bump is bad, he's
> really weird, when I see him I get
> scared . . .
>
> Oh no, no, no I wouldn't go
> Near that crazy down belo-o-ow . . .

Even Sam was amused for a minute, and forgot how serious the situation was. Only for a minute, though.

'Hang on,' she said. 'Stop it! It's not funny. I've got to get my brother *out* of there.'

'Quite right, Samantha,' said Miz T. 'It is a serious situation. I'll just feed Dog and have a look in the Books. Come. Not you, Dog.'

At the words 'feed Dog', Dog's tongue was out and ready. On 'come' she practically ran through Sam to follow

Miz Tiggle out of the parlour. Sam was left with the other Bumps. This was ridiculous. 'Feed the *dog*?' she said. 'Look in *books*? Right, I'm going to have to do this myself. How do I get out of here?'

Lorni pointed to a door next to the windows. Through them Sam saw a sunlit garden. She opened the door. No garden, just another dusty, sub-Toy Shop corridor. She hesitated just for a moment, looked back at the Bumps, then walked off into the cobwebbed unknown.

You'll have to move fast to keep up with Sam as she strides down the corridor. She's determined. She slows. She stops. There are three ways to go. Which one? Watch as she stands there and a large arm comes up behind her and a hand falls on her shoulder and Sam wheels around, smacks it away, kicks out and then realizes that she's just kicked . . . Lorni. Behind him are Creaker, Thumper, Shake Rattle and Roll.

'Don' hit me!' squeaked Lorni. 'Don' hit me! I had to follow you.'

'He was just curious,' Shake Rattle explained, edging in front of Roll. 'He's always curious. That's why they call him Snoop. *We* came to help!'

'So did us,' said Creaker.

'Posolutely,' said Thumper.

'Well, me too,' said Lorni. 'Three.'

Lorni counted the other Bumps, thought, then counted himself. 'Five,' he said. 'Me five.'

'Thank you, Lorni,' said Sam. 'Thanks, everybody. Okay, let's go!'

Everyone moved at once, and each Bump pointed in a completely different direction, and everybody said the same thing: 'This way.' 'This way.' 'This way.' 'This way.' 'This way.'

'You're supposed to be *helping* me,' said Sam. 'The Ink Thief can't be in *all* those directions. Which one is it?'

'Th-the *Ink* Thief?' Lorni stuttered. 'You don' wanna find the *Ink* Thief.' Sam's patience, which she didn't have much of at the best of times, was wearing thin. 'Yes I *do*,' she said. 'That's why we're *here*.'

'It is?' Lorni whimpered. 'Uh-oh.'

'He's got her brother,' Thumper explained. He'd been explaining this to Lorni all the way down the corridor, but he thought this might be a good time to try again.

Amazingly, this time it worked. Lorni got the picture. 'Okay. I'll show you where he is,' he said, 'but you gotta hold my hand.'

Miz Tiggle returned from feeding Dog, walked across the parlour to the bookshelf, and ran her finger along the ornate and unusual books it contained. Finally she chose one, and took it to her desk. It had an altogether wonderful cover. It looked like a collage of an Autumn forest floor. Miz Tiggle cleared some of the maps of exotic countries and star systems from the centre of her desk, and opened the Book. There was absolutely nothing in it. The pages were completely blank and yet . . . Miz T was studying them with all her attention.

'Mmm,' she said. 'Ha. Thought so. I s'pose we'll have to. Let's see.'

Watch the Book. Watch how the blank page starts to be full of shapes, colours, Bumps . . . screaming Bumps running down a corridor and now you're not looking at a moving picture in a book, you're . . .

In the corridor, with screaming, terrified Bumps running straight at you. Thumper, Creaker, Shake Rattle and Roll fall all over each other as they run by. Behind them comes

Lorni, gibbering with fear but looking back and maybe not as sure as the others that running away is the thing to do.

Whatever the terrified Bumps are running from, it's coming. There's a sound like a steel whip and here comes Sam with . . . Toddy about to catch her! He misses, and his claws make another nasty steel whip sound as they hit the wall. Finally, he has her. Sam is cornered.

Toddy's claws reached for Sam's face. 'Okay, girlie,' he panted, 'I got you now.'

'Girlie, hey?' said Sam and, as Toddy pounced, she gave him a thump on the head, and a little push, and sent him stumbling away and she ran . . . straight into Aloysius. The Rat looked far more interested in slouching and gnawing on a huge bone than in Sam, but he moved with frightening speed to catch her. Sam tried to struggle, but now Toddy was there to help Aloysius hold her.

'Here ya go, Cat,' said Aloysius. 'Take her to our leader. Make his night, nye he he he . . . ho. Uh. I don' believe it. Look what's comin' to da rescue.'

Aloysius pointed with his bone and there he was. Lorni Snoop. Coming to the rescue. He looked determined. The big hunk of quivering jelly suddenly just looked like a big hunk. He advanced on the bad Bumps like a cross between Rambo and Clint Eastwood and . . .

In the parlour, Miz Tiggle watched her Strange Book and saw Lorni stalking down the corridor to rescue Sam. She saw the creatures holding Sam. She stood. She hitched up her sleeves. She hitched up her skirt, and . . . the door burst open and Dog came charging in, yeowling and barking and whining. She almost slammed the door, then remembered not to and closed it carefully and then *howled* and whined as she ran to Miz Tiggle.

'For a Bump,' said Miz T, 'you're very doggy. I'm sure
you inspire all the real dogs in the Galaxy to do wonderfully
doggy things . . . but you *are* a Bump. You *can* talk if you
want to. So. Speak. What?'

'Ruff!' Dog barked. 'Nasty an' 'orrible an' ruff! Looka!'

Dog pointed to the closed door back out to the
corridors.

'I know,' said Miz Tiggle. 'Come.'

Miz T hitched up her skirt again. Dog hitched up her
fur. Miz T hitched up her sleeves again. Dog hitched up
her other fur. Then Miz jumped right through the closed
door in a blaze of blue light . . . followed by Dog in a blaze
of light orange.

In the creepy corridor, Lorni kept coming. He looked
serious about saving Sam from Aloysius and Toddy. Aloysius looked bored. Without turning to Toddy, he spoke to
him. 'Try the claws again,' he said, 'an' this time hit hard.'
'Hard,' said Toddy. 'Right.' 'Tear off his dingus,' Aloysius
snarled. 'His dingus,' said Toddy. 'Right!'

Toddy's claws flicked out. He advanced on Lorni and
. . . Lorni stopped. He started to sag. The excitement of
being a hero and saving Sam started to be replaced by the
more familiar feeling of terror.

'Don't be afraid, Lorni,' said Sam. 'You're a Bump.
You're imaginary. You can't get hurt.'

'Oh yes I could, I could, I could,' Lorni moaned.
'Imaginery hurting can be worse than you imagine!'

Toddy was enjoying this. Someone was actually terrified
of him. He strutted and swaggered toward Lorni. 'Yeah,'
he smirked, 'and you can't imagine worster than me!'

Toddy pounced. He landed on Lorni and flattened him.

Lorni was big enough to lift three Toddys, but his own fear knocked him down with very little actual help from Toddy. Sam struggled wildly in Aloysius' grasp, wanting to go help the frightened Bump who'd tried to help her.

'Let me go! Leave him alone, you bully!' she shouted.

'Hehhh, yeah!' Toddy giggled. 'Yeah. I'm a bully . . . an' I'm bad! Watch this.' Toddy put his paws either side of Lorni's head and batted it back and forth like a ping pong ball and . . .

Sam could take no more. With a sharp, twisting movement she broke Aloysius' grip, ran to help Lorni and . . . froze at the sight of Miz Tiggle leaping through the solid wall into the corridor. Toddy was about to thump Lorni again when he saw Miz T coming through the stones, straight at him. He stopped in mid-thump and ran to hide behind Aloysius. Aloysius didn't look bored anymore. He was giving Miz Tiggle his undivided attention.

Miz T, for her part, was paying no attention to either Rat or Cat. With Sam's help she lifted Lorni back to his feet.

'You're not a bad Bump, Lorni Snoop,' she said as she helped him up. 'Not a bad Bump at all. The OOB will be proud of you for trying to protect Samantha.'

'But I didn't protec' her,' Lorni moaned.

'Sorry, Sam. I got s-s-s-s-scared again.'

'Never mind,' said Miz T, comfortingly. 'You tried. That's the important thing. Now, speaking of Bad Bumps . . .'

Miz T turned to Toddy and Aloysius and roasted them with a look. 'Are you afraid of them?' she asked Sam.

'No,' said Sam, and you could see that she meant it.

'Right,' Miz T said. 'Come on, then.'

*

The safe place to be is behind Miz T as she and Sam walk side by side toward the two nasties and . . . *hide* as Aloysius makes a sudden move, and see him stop dead as Miz Tiggle raises both fists and lifts her leg up high enough to kick his head off. Watch closely. It's not every day you see a heroic librarian in a prim grey dress lift up a strong leg in silly stripy tights and terrify a couple of monsters. Sam is certainly watching, and you can tell that she likes what she's seeing because she copies Miz T.

Aloysius didn't like what he was seeing at all. 'All right. All right,' he said. 'I can explain.'

Sam and Miz T looked at each other. They nodded. They dropped their guards.

'We came to take the girlie to her brother,' Aloysius explained. 'Didn't we, Tod?'

'Yeah,' Toddy burbled, 'an' stick her in the machine, 'cause there's lotsa power in nasty smelly stinkin' kiddies, an' the boss needs lotsa power, 'cause then he's gonna . . .'

A large rat's paw wrapped itself across Toddy's mouth, and a big meaty bone bounced a few times off his head.

'He ain't very bright,' Aloysius smilingly explained. 'He don't understand stuff. His Bosshood just wanted the girlie to see all the fun her brother was havin' with the machine and everything. See. There he is. The little fella's havin' a great time.'

Aloysius pointed down the corridor. There, in the distance, was Jim.

Sam didn't hesitate. She ran toward him, shouting: 'Jim. Run. It's me. I'm here. It's Sam!'

Miz Tiggle shook her head, sadly, and walked after Sam. Seeing that she wasn't watching them, Toddy and Aloysius gave Lorni a last thump or three, then crept away before

Miz Tiggle noticed. As they went, Toddy did something he wasn't very good at. He thought. Then he whispered to Aloysius: 'If we're so bad, how come we're scared of Miz Tiggle?'

'I'm not scared of Miz Tiggle,' said Aloysius. 'It's the Strange Books. If you mess about with Miz Tiggle, you're messin' with the Books . . . an' there's no place to hide from the Books.'

'Ah,' said Toddy. 'Right,' he said, but you could see he didn't have the slightest idea what Aloysius was talking about.

As the monsters slipped away from Miz Tiggle and Sam, Sam was still trying to run the other way toward Jim. He wasn't all *that* far away, but it seemed as though the floor was becoming a steep hill . . . and steeper . . . and steeper . . . until finally she couldn't take another step, no matter how hard she tried. Blue energy crackled around her body like some kind of force field. Unable to get closer to Jim, she called out to him: 'Jim! Don't you hear me? Jim, you've got to get out of there. I can't get through to you. J-I-I-M!!!'

A hand rested gently on Sam's shoulder, and she turned. It was Miz Tiggle.

'I can't get through, Miz T,' Sam said. 'He's right there and I can't get to him.'

Miz T put an arm around Sam's shoulder. 'I know,' she said. 'It's something to do with dimensions. Come back to the library. We'll look in the Books.'

'I don't want to look at books,' Sam snapped. 'I don't have time to look at books. I want to get my brother out of here right away and go home. It must be getting late. Mum and Dad will . . .'

'Funny business, time,' said Miz T. 'Runs out, stands

still . . . always too much of it and not enough of it. If you want to get anything done in this universe, stick to Now. There's always just enough of that. Now, if we're going to do anything for your brother we'd better have a look in the Books. Come on.'

Sam looked back at Jim. He seemed so near. She tried again, but she couldn't get an inch closer to him. She sighed and turned away. Miz Tiggle was waiting for her. So was Lorni. He held out his hand. Sam looked at Miz T, then took Lorni's hand, and the three of them walked back down the dusty corridor.

In the Ink Thief's lair, the Thief sat at the head of his dining table. It was a long, tallow-spattered board, lit by candles set on skulls and horrible, drippy candlesticks. In the background, Jim was absorbed in the Book of the Ink Thief, and Toddy slaved over the steaming Power Machine . . . throwing in books and paintings, pulling hard on levers, turning wheels and checking the dripping of golden liquid Power into a soup bowl.

Come over to the Ink Thief's table. An antique bowl and spoon are set before the Thief. A short way down the table, Aloysius toys with a plate of bloody bones and semi-edible rubbish. Listen. They're talking about Miz Tiggle.

'Fun, though,' said the Thief, 'isn't she?'

'No,' Aloysius slobbered between chomps of bone.

'Oh, really, my dear,' the Thief sneered, 'where's your manly courage?'

'Not a man, am I?' Aloysius growled. 'Not yet.'

'No,' said the Thief, 'but you're well on the way. Have patience. I got you this far, didn't I?'

'I'm thinkin',' said Aloysius, 'that maybe this is far enough. Miz Tiggle knows the Owner. She'll use the Books.

Look at the timer.' Aloysius pointed to the Ink Timer above
the Thief's desk. It was low. The ink in the upper glass was
dripping slowly and steadily down.

'The Lease on the shop is almost up,' Aloysius said.
'Almost time for a new Thief, an' then what happens to me?
I'm happy like I am now, and I'm outa here before . . .'

'No, no, no, no, no,' the Thief crooned. 'There's time
enough. You've got it all wrong.'

Slinking from his chair, the Thief oozed over to Aloysius
and placed a companionly hand on the creature's shoulder.
'Rats desert a sinking ship, not a flying one. Yes, flying, and
make no mistake, I am rising fast. I will *be*. I have the boy.
The boy understands the Book. I can make out a bit here
and a bit there, but he *understands* it. He will gain knowledge, and his knowledge will yield Power, and the Power
will be *mine*. I will be Real at last. I will be a Man, and
more of a man than any man has ever been before. I will be
something. Imagination is nothing. Bumps are less than
nothing. And as for you . . .'

The Thief leaned further and further into Aloysius' face
as he spoke. By now the Rat was looking more than a bit
worried.

'Remember,' asked the Thief, 'when you were small?'

Aloysius nodded and tried to crawl away through the
back of his chair.

'Remember,' asked the Thief, 'when you were afraid of
cats?'

Aloysius nodded again and tried to fall through the floor.

'Want to be like that again?' the Thief enquired.

Aloysius smiled sheepishly and quivered with fear as the
Thief ran an awful hand along his face. 'Then don't cross
me,' the Thief hissed. 'Ah, lunch.'

The Thief returned to his place at the head of the table
just as Toddy began to serve Power from the Power

Machine. He ladled the golden liquid into the Thief's bowl. The Thief controlled himself. With every nerve straining to pour the whole bowl down his throat, he lifted the spoon and supped delicately. His eyes widened. Energy crackled around him and he seemed to grow in his chair as . . . In another chair, at the Ink Thief's desk, Jim sat in a pool of candlelight. He mumbled as he turned the huge pages.

'Nothing equals everything,' he said to himself. 'Everything comes from Nothing. It's sub-quantum physics, and it's so simple.' He turned another page. 'I knew it. It *will* work. We *can* change the world.'

A brighter glow than the candles began to shine from the Book, bathing Jim in a corona of light. As he stood and turned, the light blazed around him like a sunrise. Jim was inspired. 'Yes!' he exclaimed. 'We can do it!'

The Thief, sitting at his table, watched Jim with fascination. The Thief stood. He approached Jim. He too was inspired. 'Power!' he cried.

'We can have peace!' said Jim.

'Power!!' howled the Thief.

'Happiness!' Jim laughed.

'Power!!!' shrieked the Thief.

'Perfection!' said Jim.

'Power!!!!' screamed the Thief.

'Infinite Power,' said Jim with quiet satisfaction.

'Oh, we *do* speak the same language,' chortled the Thief. 'Not quite the same meaning, but never mind. You'll learn.'

Through the window of Miz Tiggle's parlour, the sun was setting. Miz T and Sam sat at a small table, drinking tea. Miz Tiggle refilled their cups from the teapot. This was not easy, because Dog kept shoving her big red bowl in and banging it on the table and begging and trying to steal cakes. Finally, Dog got her tea. Delicately, like a person, she took milk and a tiny bit of sugar and then . . . when Miz T wasn't looking . . . she poured *all* the sugar into her bowl and flopped down on all fours on the floor and slurped her tea from the bowl like a dog.

Neither Miz T nor Sam paid any attention to all this. They had serious problems to solve.

'Well, it's not as though you have to stay here,' said Miz T. 'You can go home any time you want to.'

'We can?' Sam asked, surprised.

'You can,' said Miz T. 'He can't. I said you could go home any time you *want* to. James doesn't want to.'

'Right,' said Sam. 'Then I will. Show me the way out. I'll get my mum and dad and the police, and we'll all come back here and . . .'

'And they won't find a thing,' said Miz T. 'Just a dusty old toy shop with no one in it.'

'What?' Sam asked. 'Why?'

Miz T was ready with her usual explanation: 'It's something to do with dimensions.'

Sam paused. She thought. Miz Tiggle sipped her tea. Dog climbed up on her chair and joined the party. Finally Miz Tiggle stood, went to her desk, and returned carrying the big book with the wonderful cover. Sam stared at it. 'What a strange book,' she said.

'Precisely,' Miz T agreed, and showed her what was written on the spine.

There, in letters which seemed to move and change colours, were the words: 'Strange Books – Vol.1.' Miz T opened the book in front of Sam. There was nothing on the first page. Carefully, Sam leafed through it. The whole thing consisted of blank pages.

'How?' inquired Sam, 'is an empty book going to help me get my brother back? And *please* don't say it's something to do with dimensions!'

'All right,' Miz T agreed, 'I won't . . . but it is. Let's see, late twentieth century. Computers, right? No storage missing in *my* attic. Computer screen's got nothing on it 'til you turn it on. It's just space to show things in. Strange Books are like that. Nothin' in 'em so you can have anything in 'em you want.'

'Anything?' asked Sam.

'Anything you want.'

'I want to see what Jim's doing.'

Miz T agreed. 'So do I.'

Miz T moved to sit next to Sam, with the Book in front of them. 'Right,' she said. 'Well. Now. To use the Books you have to pay . . .'

Dog interrupted Miz T by leaping onto the chair next to her and fixing on the book like a pointer concentrating on a bird. Miz T held her back and said: 'Not you, Samantha. As I was saying . . .'

'I've only got pocket money with me,' Sam interrupted. 'I could get . . .'

'Not money,' said Miz T. 'Attention. You have to pay attention.'

Sam looked relieved. 'Oh. Good,' she said. 'I can do that.'

'Me too,' barked Dog. 'Pay 'tension and have 'ventures. Ruff!'

'All right, then,' said Miz T, 'give it all the attention you've got and watch what happens.'

Lean in close with Dog and Sam. Watch Miz T's hands turning the empty pages, and Dog's paws helping, and . . . ghosts of moving pictures fading up into . . .

The Ink Thief's lair. There's Jim with the Thief at the big desk and here's Toddy replacing the soup bowl under the Power outlet of the Machine. Keeping his position as World's Most Clumsy Cat, he stumbles as he stands and bangs into the Machine. It gurgles and, to Toddy's great delight, a couple of lingering drops of Power are dislodged from the system. Toddy looks around to be sure no one's watching him.

People are watching, but Toddy can't see them. It's Miz T, Sam and Dog appearing right in front of him. Toddy takes no notice.

'Don't worry,' said Miz T. 'They can't see us.'

'There's Jim,' said Sam. 'Jim!' 'Can't hear us either,' Miz T explained.

Follow Sam, Miz T and Dog as they go toward Jim and watch with them as Jim and the Ink Thief work with the Book. It pours light around them like something from a Steven Spielberg movie. Candles flicker on skulls. Yuck bubbles in jars. Sam watches all of this with increasing anger, and listens as Jim says: 'People are hungry. There are wars everywhere, and the planet is a mess . . . and here's enough Power to change it all.' The Thief gives thanks, apparently to the ceiling. 'He understands. The boy understands!'

It was obvious that Jim did understand the book. 'Things can be perfect,' he said. 'We have infinite Power, we just didn't know it.'

'And now we do?' asked the Thief gleefully. 'We do,' said Jim.

'We DO!' the Thief echoed.

'It's easy,' said Jim.

'*Easy!*' cried the Thief.

'Heaven and Earth,' Jim exclaimed.

'Yesss!' the Thief hissed, 'and Imagination can go to hell!

No more imagining myself. Look out real world, here I come!'

Sam could listen to no more of her brother playing games with this crazy person . . . thing . . . Bump . . . whatever he was. Before they could stop her, she was away from Miz T and Dog and had gone right up to Jim and the Thief. 'Oh, Jim, you silly twaddle,' she shouted at him, 'wake up! *Look* at him. Look at this place. It's like Frankenstein meets the Phantom.'

Sam was only in the lair through the Strange Book. Her body was still back in Miz T's parlour. Jim couldn't see her. He couldn't hear her, and yet . . . he suddenly looked puzzled, as though he was trying to work something out.

The Thief caught the change in mood. He was concerned. 'What is it, boy?' he asked Jim.

'Well, it's only . . .' said Jim thoughtfully, 'that there's all kinds of things you can do with power, and this *is* all a bit like something out of a Frankenstein movie . . . no offence, of course, but I can't help noticing . . .'

Miz T had pulled Sam back to stay near her and Dog. Now she looked strangely at Sam and then the scene in front of them. 'It's as though he heard you,' she said. 'Hmmm . . .'

Miz T looked puzzled. The Thief also looked puzzled. What to say to the boy? Of course, the place looked like something out of a Frankenstein movie. The Thief prided himself on his horribly good taste. 'Frankenstein . . .' he said. 'The Phantom, Faust . . . these are not monsters. They're not evil people. They're heroes. They want us to have greatness, to reach for the stars. It's the Miz Tiggles who hold people down, who want things to be as they are. Just because we're unusual, they make up stories about science being evil . . . and people believe them. Do you want things to be as they are? Hunger, war . . .'

'Never again,' said Jim.

'And you won't turn against me,' the Thief asked, 'because of my horrible taste in clothes and furniture?'

'Ridiculous,' Jim said.

'Then we *will* change the world,' the Thief whispered. 'Come, let's drink to it.'

Miz T, Sam and Dog could only watch.

'I don't believe this,' Sam said.

'Unfortunately,' Miz T replied, 'Jim does.'

Toddy has made a wonderful discovery. Thumping and kicking different bits of the Power Machine gets left-over drops of Power out of the system. Toddy never gets enough Power. He hardly gets enough to keep being a cat, let alone a person. This is his big chance. No one's looking. Power for Toddy! He's thumping and kicking for all he's worth, checking the level of power in the soup bowl, going back to thump out just one more drop and returning to find . . . the Thief, holding his bowl of Power.

'Ah, Toddy,' says the Thief. 'Go get Aloysius. We're going to drink a toast.'

Toddy looks at the bowl of Power, almost reaches for it, looks peeved, looks dismayed, looks angry, then looks for Aloysius. He spots the Rat across the chamber, and trundles toward him. He is not a happy cat.

Aloysius was asleep at the table, his huge arms curled around the even huge-er bone he used for nibbling on when he was slightly munchy and hitting Toddy with most of the rest of the time. Toddy walked straight to Aloysius, looked *really* sad, and lay his head on the sleeping Rat's shoulder. Aloysius snorted. He snuffled. He woke up, saw

Toddy cuddled up on him and gave him a sharp whap on the head with the bone and Toddy remembered: 'The Boss wants us to drink some toast.'

'*A* toast,' said Aloysius.

'I don' care *how* much toast,' Toddy whined. 'I had a whole puddle of Power all for me, an' now the 'orrible stinky kid gets it, and I gets toast!'

'Puddle' and 'power', the way Toddy said them, were spitty sort of words. Aloysius had to wipe the Toddy-spit out of his eye before he could say: 'Nah, cat. A toast means we all gets to drink the Power. C'mon.'

Toddy was so excited by this news that he tried to climb over Aloysius, then tried to run around him, then broke all sprint records for clumsy cats, returning to his Master right behind Aloysius and just in time for the toast. The Thief raised the soup bowl, which was glowing with golden Power. He offered the toast. It was one word: 'Power!'

The Thief drank. He glowed. He crackled. He passed the bowl to Jim.

'Power!' said Jim, putting the bowl to his lips and pouring in the Power. His eyes brightened. His body glowed. Energy crackled around him as he handed the bowl to Aloysius.

'Power!' roared Aloysius, and blazed as he swallowed the stuff. Toddy, ignored, had to pull the container from his hands. He tried to drink. He looked inside the bowl. He turned it upside down. It was empty. Furious, Toddy turned on the other three.

'What about me?' he moaned. 'What about me? What about ME!?'

'You?' said Aloysius, bopping Toddy again with his bone club. 'You could make us some toast . . . nye he he he he he.'

The Thief didn't see any of this. He was watching Jim. Jim, crackling with Power, had gone to the Book of the Ink Thief. The Book was shining. Jim was shining. Suddenly, he turned to the Thief. 'There are other books,' Jim said. 'Strange Books.'

'I know,' the Thief replied.

'They're watching us,' said Jim.

Miz Tiggle was astonished, and it showed. 'He can't know that,' she said.

'But he does,' said Sam.

Look at the Thief, snaking toward Jim. He's delighted. He's almost in awe as he says: 'It's Tiggle. She wants to stop us. What shall we do, boy?'

Jim says nothing. He smiles. He reaches his hand out and it disappears, sinking into invisibility up to the elbow . . . the shoulder and . . .

Go to Miz Tiggle, Sam and Dog. Miz T is even more surprised than the Thief. 'I don't believe it,' she says. 'Hold on tight.'

Hold on tight, and watch as the scene in the lair begins to fade and . . .

Miz T, Sam and Dog were suddenly back at the parlour table with the Strange Book. Stranger than the Book, though, was what was now happening to it. Jim's arm was reaching into the room out of nowhere. His small hand was grasping the Book. He pulled and . . . Miz T pulled back. So did Sam. Dog pulled on Sam and . . . people and Book all landed on Dog.

'Frathersnaggits!' Miz T exclaimed. 'Lot of Power in that brother of yours.'

In a corner of the Ink Thief's lair, Toddy was looking very upset indeed. Turning to Aloysius, he poured out his heart. 'There's no Power for Toddy,' he complained. 'No, no Power for me, an' I do all the work, an' the nasty stinkin' kid gets the Power, an' how'm I suppose to be a bad cat if I don' have any Power, an' I'm just mad!'

He was. Mad. Also sad. He buried his unhappy face in the Rat's hairy, leathery, metal-studded and chain-draped chest. Awww. Didums pussycat. Aloysius stroked him for a moment . . . then bounced his head off the studs and chains. 'I got no sympathy for you at all cat,' he snarled. 'I've told you and I've told you: Don't get mad, get evil!'

Toddy looked at the Thief, absorbed with Jim, and a wonderfully nasty expression spread across his face.

'Nyaarrr!' he chortled evilly.

'Harrr!' Aloysius replied, and laughed an evil laugh, and Toddy laughed an evil laugh . . . and Aloysius smacked him again with the bone just to show that he still didn't have any sympathy at all.

CHAPTER THREE

Nasty and the OOB

Beams of coloured sunlight were shining through the stained-glass windows, but Sam's expression was dark as she followed Miz Tiggle and Dog across the Reading Room.

'I *hate* him,' Sam said.

'Won't help,' said Miz T. 'Get that trolley. Not you, Dog.'

Dog bounced and waggled her way to the book trolley and wheeled it, jumped on it and rode it the few metres back to Miz Tiggle.

'I'm gonna fight him,' said Sam.

'You'll lose,' Miz T replied while stacking scrolls from the trolley into Dog's arms.

Miz Tiggle's calm was making Sam boiling mad. Now she boiled over. 'I've had *enough*!' she said, pushing in between Dog and Miz T. 'I want my brother *out* of there! The Books are supposed to give me what I want. What's the problem?'

Miz Tiggle's response was to stop handing scrolls to Dog, and start handing them to Sam . . . who handed them to Dog because she wasn't interested in being a librarian, she was interested in getting her brother back. Dog was left to juggle a growing pile of scrolls in her arms while her head flipped from Sam to Miz T, trying to follow their conversation.

'The problem,' Miz T told Sam, 'is that you don't actually know what you want. Confuses the Books. It's like pressing lots of keys at once on one of your computer thingies. Scrambles it all up.'

"But I *do* know what I want,' Sam replied, taking yet another scroll and adding it to the high, shaky pile in Dog's arms.

'You think you do,' said Miz T.

'I *know* I do,' said Sam.

'Then the Books ought to work.'

'Then they will.'

'They won't.'

'I *do* know.'

'You don't.'

Dog watched this exchange like a tennis match, her head swivelling from one side of the net to the other. As the speed increased, it looked like her tongue and eyeballs were going to fly off in opposite directions.

'I don't care about the Books,' said Sam. 'I'll save Jim myself!'

'You will,' said Miz T.

'I will!'

'You will.'

'I will! I will??'

Dog has had an attack of the dizzies from moving her head backwards and forwards fast enough to follow all this.

'You've got all the power in the world,' said Miz T. 'More than the Thief could ever steal. Trouble is, you don't know how to use it. You think you want to get *away* from problems.'

'What's wrong with that?' asked Sam.

'Problems', Miz T replied, 'are how we learn. Problems are how we grow up. Trick is to get into problems, not run away from 'em. Now, think about it. What's your problem?'

'That horrible creep', said Sam, 'keeping my brother down there.'

'Then learn about him,' Miz T advised. 'Find out what you're up against. There's no free lunches, girl. Do your homework.'

'I hate homework,' Sam snapped.

'You want James back?' asked Miz T.

Sam sighed. 'I'll do homework,' she said. 'What do I do?'

Miz T turned, and began to walk away in the direction of the parlour. As she went she gave instructions. 'For a start, you want to understand the Thief. See where he's coming from. Move that trolley over to stack number .00B00.'

Dog, who had finally got over the dizzies and was just getting comfortable on the trolley, struggled to get off it. 'Not Dog,' Miz T explained to Sam, 'you. I'll be right back.' Sam took hold of the trolley and pushed it along, looking for .00B00 on the numbered shelves. Dog lay back and enjoyed the ride and . . .

Over Jim's shoulder you can see the Book of the Thief. It will take a moment to get used to the inky, intricate style and . . . wait. Jim has noticed something. There's writing along the bound edge of the page, at a right angle to the text. Below the writing there's a line of dots. Jim tries to turn the Book to read this strange addition. He can't. The Book is incredibly heavy. Unable to move it, Jim moves himself. He climbs up on the desk and kneels in the right direction to read along the binding. He looks very surprised. Without getting up there with him we don't know what's astonished him, nor why he mumbles: 'That can't be right.'

Jim wiggles back down to the chair. He leafs quickly back and forth through the nearest pages of the Book and doesn't see what we see, which is . . .

Toddy, creeping toward him out of the gloom. Toddy's expression is not nice at all as he says: 'I'm not gonna get mad, I'm gonna get evil, an' I'm gonna get that 'orrible stinkin' kid!'

Whatever Jim has discovered in the Book, it's got him jumping with excitement. He doesn't notice anything as Toddy creeps up on him. Toddy raises his paws and stalks Jim. Thwock! . . . the claws come out as Jim climbs back up on the desk to read the sideways writing again and . . . Thunk! . . . Jim's moving makes Toddy miss and one set of claws go into the desk and he can't pull them free so he strikes with the other hand and Jim doesn't even notice and goes running off excitedly and Toddy misses again and the other set of claws get stuck . . . and Toddy is left with his arms crossed and his claws stuck in the wood, feeling angry and stupid and sad all at once and . . .

In the library, Miz Tiggle was back from the parlour with a Strange Book under her arm. She dropped it on a reading table, and the thump echoed around the big room.

'Samantha,' she called out, 'where have you got to?'

Sam's voice sounded near, but there was no sign of her as she said: 'That's what I'd like to know. Wherever I am, there's a lot of books floating around. Dog says it's something screwy, but I don't . . . oh!'

Out of nowhere, Sam faded into the room. She was sitting on the book trolley, and being pushed along by Dog. 'What was all *that*?' she asked the universe in general.

'Screwy dooies,' said Dog.

'What happened?' Miz T asked.

'Well,' Sam said, 'you told me to take the trolley to .00B00, so I followed the signs, and turned a corner, and bang . . . floating books. No library.'

Surprisingly, Miz T was not surprised. 'You'll get used to it,' she said. 'It's the Screwy Decimal System. Organizes all the imagination in the Books. Does funny things to space. And time. And speaking of time, it's time to do your homework.'

'I hate that word,' Sam grumbled.

'Time?' asked Miz T.

'No. Homework. Jim loves it. I hate it.'

'Nothing wrong with you two that being a bit like each other wouldn't fix,' Miz T declared. 'Sit. Dog *and* you.'

Miz Tiggle sat down with the book. Sam and Dog joined her.

'Now,' said Miz T. 'Ink Thieves. Nothing wrong with your basic Ink Thief. Good profession for a boy. Bump. Whatever. This one just made a small mistake, and it got out of hand. He's not really evil. Least I hope he's not. Have to get rid of him if he was evil. Wouldn't be too happy about getting rid of him.'

'Why?' asked Sam. 'He's nasty, he's selfish, he's horrible . . .'

'It's personal,' Miz T sniffed. 'You don't have to know everything. Well, you do, but . . . Anyhow. Ink Thieves.'

Miz Tiggle opens the Strange Book. Sam and Dog lean forward with her. Lean in with them and watch as the empty page fills with a moving scene and suddenly, without actually going anywhere . . .

Miz Tiggle, Sam and Dog stood in the Ink Thief's lair . . . sort of. It looked different. It was relatively tidy. There was no Toddy, no Aloysius. There *was* an Ink Thief . . . but he was dressed like an ordinary Victorian clerk and he wasn't bald and nasty looking and . . .

'He's got *hair*,' Sam whispered. 'And the place isn't filthy . . . and . . .'

'Book's showing you the Thief before the present one,' said Miz T. 'They don't last long. Sometimes only a few centuries. Job wears 'em out.'

'You mean they get tired of being such horrible creeps?' Sam asked.

'He's packing his tools to go to work,' said Miz T. 'Come on. See what Ink Thievin's all about. I mean *real* Ink Thievin'.'

In a curtained study, a philosopher stands at a high desk, writing by the light of a single candle. He thinks. He dips his quill pen in the ink well. He stops. He thinks again. Gazing into space, he stares right through Sam, Miz Tiggle and Dog as they fade into his chamber.

Sam whispers to Miz T: 'Who's that?'

'There's no need to whisper,' Miz T replied. 'He can't hear you. That's Rene Descartes. Well-known philosopher. Said: "I think, therefore I am." Famous for it. Thinking, I mean. Don't you go to school?'

'Yes, I do,' said Sam, 'and I've heard of Descartes, but how was I supposed to recognize . . .'

Descartes was perspiring, and chewing on his pen in frustration. He kept looking at a piece of paper tacked to the wall. On it were phrases crossed out and replaced by others: 'I shrink', 'I'm pink', 'I blink', 'I sink' . . . He sniffed the air. His nose wrinkled. Suddenly, with the quill wet and ragged and ink dripping everywhere, he was inspired. He lifted his pen triumphantly and cried out: 'Yes! Ja! Da! Oui! Si! C'est ça! I . . . *stink*, therefore I am! Ha! This is the big one. Write it down. I S-t-i-n-k, therefore . . . mmm. I don't know . . . Tough game, philosophy. Still, I suppose someone's got to do it. Let's see . . . I drink? I wink? Drink sounds good. Have a pot of tea. Take a break. Thanks, don't mind if I do.'

Descartes pottered out of the room and . . . the old, not-a-horrible-creep Ink Thief came in through the window. With a strange instrument, he drew the ink off the philosopher's page. He looked at the liquid. He listened to it. He tasted it. He touched it . . . and power crackled from his finger to the ink. The old Thief dropped the resulting ink into the philosopher's ink well, then slipped out the window just as Descartes returned. The philosopher put down his tea-tray. He dipped his pen in the Ink-Thief-powered ink, touched the tip absentmindedly to his lips, and got ready for an afternoon of hard philosophizing. 'I th-i-ink . . .' he said, and . . . inspiration hit him like a ton of books. His knees buckled, his eyes widened and he shouted: 'I think! I *think*! That's *it*! I *think*, therefore I am! I knew stink wasn't right. True, but not right. Mmm. There's a good one. What is the difference between true and . . .'

The rest was lost as Sam, Dog and Miz T faded out of the scene . . . and faded back, but they weren't with Descartes anymore. They were in a painter's studio. Leonardo da Vinci stood before a half-painted Mona Lisa. The Mona Lisa is a famous painting, so Sam had no trouble recognizing it.

'That's the Mona Lisa!' said Sam. 'And that's Leonardo da Vinci! Look. He's painting the famous . . . frown?'

Da Vinci had, in fact, painted a frown. In increasingly fast motion he tried replacing the frown with a silly grin, a wide-open mouth, a tongue sticking out, and finally the frown again. At last he dropped his brush on to his work table, sighed, and stood there staring at the painting and looking lost while, behind him . . . the old Ink Thief came through the wall into the room. He picked up the paintbrush. He looked at the paint, sniffed it, listened to it, tasted it, zapped it with Power, and stood back as Leonardo reached for his brush once more. The brush tingled. Leonardo tingled. His expression changed. His eyes lit up. He went to the canvas and painted the famous smile. Leonardo smiled. The old Ink Thief smiled. Sam smiled . . . and faded away . . . and . . .

Sam and Miz T were back in front of the blank Strange Book. Sam looked around, saw where she was, and saw that something was missing. 'Where's Dog?' she asked.

'Probably following the old Ink Thief around,' said Miz T. 'She likes him.'

Sam smiled. 'So did I,' she said. 'He was really sweet and he helped important people.'

'Helped everybody,' said Miz T. 'Kids with homework, grownups learning to read and write, everybody. *That's* Ink Thievin'.'

'Then how come the creep downstairs is such a horrible, slimy, nasty . . . creep?' Sam wondered.

'Imagination,' said Miz T. 'Greatest power there is. Starts out as Bumps, becomes ideas, and before you know it you've got the whole world.'

'So?' said Sam, not completely following this.

'So,' Miz T continued, 'if imagination is the greatest power, and you know how to collect the stuff because you're an Ink Thief, you could make a big mistake. Imagination makes the world happen. You start trying to steal it all for your little self, and what do you think happens to the world?'

'Trouble,' said Sam.

'Correct,' Miz T replied. 'It wasn't so bad when it started.

The OOB was worried about the new Thief stealing Power, but he wasn't very good at it. Not at first.'

'I still don't know what the OOB . . .' Sam began.

'One thing at a time,' said Miz T. 'Thief first, OOB later. Watch.'

Miz T pointed again to the Strange Book and Sam watched and moving pictures began to form and . . .

Sam and Miz T see the present day Thief, the one Sam knows and hates, the one who has her brother. It *is* him, but . . . he doesn't look so Gothic-Horrible and . . . he looks younger and . . . his clothes aren't as tattered and nasty looking. He sits at his desk, and even the desk looks fairly clean.

This is the Thief when he was younger . . . and cleaner. What he doesn't seem to have been was happier. Watch the little muscles twitching around his mouth and eyes. He rocks ever so slightly in his chair and . . . picks up an ink pot and flings it at the wall. A quill pen flies from his hand and strikes quivering, point first like an arrow, into the centre of the ink stain and the Thief howls: 'Fools! Idiots! Imaginary boobies! Offer them Everything, and they want Nothing.'

The Thief goes to a mirror. He admires himself. 'Style,' he says, and tears off his jacket. With a penknife, he cuts slits through his shirt front. He picks up a paper-wrapped parcel and tears into it, pulling out a long black vampire-style cape. He puts it on. It swirls. He admires his reflection again. His eyes blaze and he whispers to himself: 'Power!'

Follow the Thief as he storms over to a large cloth bag. He half-carries, half-throws it across the room, pulls objects out and stacks them up. Books, paintings, sculpture . . . and all the time he's still raving to himself: 'And then there's this . . . the height of stupidity . . . a machine to *give* Power to people. As though they didn't have enough already. *They're* not just imaginary. *They* don't have to work their imaginations to the bone getting everything to happen out of nothing. *They* run the world while we *Bumps* sweat over a hot imagination to make sure there's a world for them to run. Slaves, that's what we are. We? Did I say we? No more. Never again!'

The Thief goes to the Power Machine. He's getting wilder all the time. He laughs. It's not a nice sound.

'Now it's time to turn things around,' he leers, 'starting with this stupid machine. Plenty of imagination stored up in ink and paint. Now what happens if I do everything backwards? I don't increase the imagination in things . . . I steal the Power *from* the imagination in things. I put a book in the wrong end . . . so. Run the Machine *backwards* . . . so . . .'

The Thief turns handles, pulls levers, and the Machine comes to life. It smokes. It shudders, and . . . golden drops of Power drip out. The Thief runs to the outlet. The Power drips onto his hands. He tastes it. He lets the Power cover his fingers, rubs it on to his face, licks it off his fingers . . . and laughs . . . and laughs . . . and laughs.

Sam and Miz Tiggle, watching invisibly through the Strange Book, were not enjoying this performance.

'Weird,' was Sam's opinion.

'Can't say I enjoy seeing it again,' said Miz Tiggle, 'but watch. It gets worse.'

The Thief sucked the last dregs of Power off the tips of his fingers. He glowed and buzzed with the stuff.

'They're right, of course,' he snarled. 'I don't belong in the OOB. Style-free bunch of imaginary morons. I'm free at last. Free to be *something*. No more absurd rules. No more Screwy Decimal System. Throw me out of the OOB? Ha! They couldn't keep me in!'

The Thief dug into his pile of stolen books and works of art and began to stuff and crush his loot into the Power Machine. 'Silly job, Ink Thief,' he ranted to himself. 'Being a Bump . . . helping mankind . . . Pfui! *Being* a man, that's the stuff. Having Power. One day you wake up and you're an Ink Thief. Whose idea was that? Certainly not *my* idea of a good time. You get a crummy toy shop and a few thousand years to help people, and what's in it for me? Abso-stinkin'-lutely nothing!'

The Thief started the Machine. He pulled levers, turned handles, grabbed a cup and placed it under an outlet.

'Well, here's one Bump whose going to have it all!' he cackled. 'My cup runneth over!'

The Machine chuntered, steamed, and golden Power trickled into the cup. The Thief raised the glowing Power to his black lips. 'Here's to the perfection of style, charm and individual . . . thingyness,' he said. 'To me!' He drank. He crackled and glowed and . . . a rat walked across the floor of the lair. The Thief watched it, as thoughtfully as his blazing brain would permit and . . . something else caught his attention. It was a cat, heading in vaguely the same direction as the rat.

The Thief thought hot thoughts. You could tell he was thinking them by the Power-coloured steam coming off his sizzling bald head. 'Friends,' he said, watching the rat and the cat. 'Companions. Servants. Creatures who will do what I inky well tell them. Run the Machine. Frighten visitors. Thump Bumps. Appreciate my wit and conversation. Yes. I think I like it. Hello, kitty. Nice kitty.'

The Thief rushed to a sideboard. He cut a piece of cheese and threw it in a bowl. A second bowl got some milk. Bowls in hand, the Thief returned to the Machine outlet and scooped a cup of Power into each. He placed them on the floor and . . . The cat edged up to the bowl of Power-laced milk and began to drink and . . . the rat found the Power-soaked cheese and ate it as fast as it could.

Sam and Miz Tiggle were still watching all this, through the Strange Book.

'Poor little animals,' Sam said.

'Bumps,' Miz Tiggle corrected. 'They're Bumps.'

'Poor little Bumps,' said Sam, and watched as . . . The cat seemed to fade, and flicker, and glow with Power, and change, and become something else: It was *Toddy*. He looked confused. The rat went through the same changes as he became Aloysius, but Aloysius did not look confused. He looked very pleased, in a frightening sort of way. He looked down at his huge body and tried his big fists. 'Wicked,' he bellowed. For the first time, the world heard Aloysius laugh. It was tremendous. It was the sort of sound that can make a world very n-n-n-nervous. The Thief was fascinated. He watched with delight as the rat went over to the cat. Aloysius was now *much* bigger than Toddy, and the change in size seemed to amuse the rat no end.

'Well how about that, cat?' Aloysius rumbled. 'We look like people, only you're a shrimp . . . nye he he he he he!'

The Thief couldn't have been more pleased as he approached his new companions. Aloysius saw him coming. 'Uh-oh,' he said to Toddy. 'Get back. Paws for thought. It's the King Rat. Salivations, your Nastiness.' Toddy was still confused, but he was also delighted. He ran to the Thief. 'I'm a people,' he burbled. 'Toddy da Cat is a people! Oh tanks, yer Bossness. I'll do anything you ask.'

'Will you work for me?' the Thief asked.

'Yuss!' said Toddy.

'Will you steal for me?'

'Yuss!'

'Will you fight the OOB to the bitter end for me?'

'Y—'

Aloysius pushed Toddy aside before he could answer. 'I'm yer rat for that, yer Awfulness,' he rumbled. 'Ol' Toddy here's not very tough. Has his good points though, for a cat.'

'Such as?' the Thief enquired.

'Well, he's clumsy,' said Aloysius, 'and he's kinda stupid.'

'I ain't,' said Toddy.

'You is,' Aloysius replied.

'I ain't.'

'You is.'

'I ain't.'

'You is. You know what a Twinkie is?' Aloysius enquired.

'Uh-uh,' Toddy whined.

'It's a fluffy cake full of squidge,' said Aloysius. 'Cat, you're a Twinkie.'

Toddy turned to the Thief. 'Don' listen to him, your Bossness,' he growled. 'Toddy's a *bad* cat. I'll get that OOB for ya. I'll pouncify 'em. I'll scratch their scrungles. I'll *grobelize* 'em.' The Thief patted Toddy on the head, and Toddy swelled with badness and pride and stuck out his tongue at Aloysius.

Sam and Miz Tiggle had watched all this in silence. Now Sam spoke. 'I think it's time somebody told me what the OOB is,' she said.

'You're spendin' the evening with 'em,' Miz T replied, 'but first you need to watch this bit.' Miz Tiggle pointed back to the Thief and his new servants and Sam watched as . . .

The Thief placed a fresh bowl of Power on his desk and pointed dramatically toward the Power Machine. 'You see that pile of books and paintings?' he asked.

'Yeah!' said Toddy, 'I got eyes like a cat!'

'Consider it seen,' Aloysius replied.

'I stole them,' said the Thief, 'with my own, interesting hands. Now you will steal for me. Books, paintings, music, anything with Imagination in it. It will all go in the Machine, and from the Imagination we will drain out . . . Power! A great deal of Power. Enough Power to make us Real. I will be a Bump no more. I will be a Man.'

The Thief drank deeply from the fresh bowl of Power. He glowed, he crackled with the stuff, he blazed. 'The real world will be mine!' he hissed. 'No more being Imagination. Man is the ruler, and I will be a Man such as the world has not yet seen.'

The Thief raised the bowl again. Toddy and Aloysius drooled expectantly, but the Thief drained it himself. He seemed to be getting a bit, well . . . drunk. He threw the empty bowl to Toddy, who caught it out of pure self-defence. 'Fire up the Machine!' the Thief shouted. 'Fling in all that cultural rubbish,' he cried. 'Get every drop of Power out of every book, every painting, every piece of artistic nonsense,' he chortled, pointing to the pile of loot. 'Let's have another pot of Power! Let's have a few! The aeon is young!'

A mad grin spread across Aloysius' face. 'Ey,' he shouted. 'Turn on the Power, cat. Let's party!'

Toddy was a willing servant. Power sounded good. So did party. He threw the stuff in by the armful. 'Now . . . turn all the wheels,' the Ink Thief called. 'Pull all the levers! One at a time. Yes . . . go on . . . ah! What a beautiful sight.'

Power began to flow. Toddy filled the bowl. The Thief

drank it. He filled another. Aloysius chugged it down. He filled a third. The Thief poured it down his throat and the front of his clothes. Finally Toddy went to fill the bowl for himself and . . . the flow had stopped. Toddy was peeved. He slumped . . . and then he saw . . . a big book lying behind the machine. He looked around carefully to make sure no one was watching, slipped the book silently into the Machine, worked his way quietly down the wheels and levers and . . . lay down under the outlet with his mouth wide open, letting the power pour in.

At his desk, the Thief was totally pickled on Power. Aloysius was falling about, drunk out of his small Rat mind. The Thief stood on his desk. From this commanding height, he surveyed his underground kingdom. 'You, my fine rat,' he pronounced, 'will give the operation the right quality of vicious nastiness. The cat will do for a dim, strange servant. I have seen the future . . . and it is me!'

With these words the Thief fell off his desk onto Aloysius, and the two of them slid to the ground. The Thief giggled. Aloysius giggled, and . . .

Sam and Miz T watched. Sam was puzzled. 'They're acting like they're drunk,' she said. 'It's easy to get drunk on Power,' said Miz T, and it was clear that she did not approve.

The Thief couldn't have cared less. He was having fun. He reached for another bag of books and pulled one out. 'Cat!' he shouted.

Toddy had finally got to drink lots of Power. Now he was leaning up against the Machine, an idiot grin on his face, burbling and giggling to himself. At the sound of his Master's voice he looked blearily around . . . and smacked into a flying book. 'More Power!' the Thief yelled, and threw another one. Aloysius joined in, pulling books from the sack and flinging them at Toddy. Toddy stumbled around, putting books in the Machine, draining out the Power, getting hit by books, catching books. After a bit the Thief left Aloysius to have the fun of throwing things at Toddy, while he himself sat there on the floor, drinking and bathing in Power.

Toddy, meanwhile, had been hit by a book about fish. It was full of pictures and Toddy was in love with it. He wanted to eat it. He let the books Aloysius was throwing smack into him as he dribbled on the fishies and . . .

At his desk, the Thief was back on his feet. He was shining with Power. He lifted the glowing bowl. He proposed the Terrible Toast: 'Today', he cried, 'the Toy Shop! Tomorrow . . . the World!'

Toddy watched his Master. He was inspired. 'Today', he purred, 'fish. Tomorrow . . . fish!'

Sam was surprised to see Toddy swirl like smoke and begin to drift away, along with the Ink Thief, Aloysius and the lair. She found herself floating in streaming colours and flickering shapes. Miz T seemed to be concentrating on something, and paying no attention to the strange surroundings.

'What's happening?' Sam asked. 'Where are we?'

'Between time and space,' Miz T replied. 'I'm fast-forwarding the Book. Most of this is pretty boring. The Thief gets good at being the selfishness Bump, the servants get good at being nasty and stupid . . . it's an old story, and

I don't like it enough to watch the whole thing again. Ah
. . . better see this bit.'

Through the streaming colours, the Ink Thief's lair returns.
Time has clearly passed. This is the dark and horrible lair
Sam knows and doesn't love. She watches as Toddy pulls a
very heavy sack of books to the Power Machine. Like a
steam engine stoker in hell, he sweats over the levers and
wheels and loading and . . . the Thief paces. He measures
power. He consults the Book. He goes to the Ink Timer
and stares at it, lost in thought. Aloysius comes in, goes to
the Thief, waits, gets no reply, makes throat-clearing noises,
gets no response, and finally speaks: ''Scuse me, yer
'orribleness.'

The Thief didn't look pleased to be interrupted. 'Mmm?
Yes? What?' he snarled.

   ''They're back,' said Aloysius.

   'And . . .?' the Thief prompted.

   'They want us out,' said Aloysius.

   'Again?' the Thief asked, as if this was the most boring
news of the millennium. 'Tell them there's still ink in the
Timer. Tell them the Owner can't have this place back until
the Timer runs out. Tell them I'll soon have enough Power
to be Real, and then . . . No. Don't tell them anything. I
think I'll show them. Is it the whole OOB?'

   'Most of 'em,' Aloysius replied.

   'Good,' the Thief said, and took a measure of Power
from his desk. He raised it to his lips and drained it. Then,
wild-eyed and radiating Power, he went to the main door
of the lair and threw it open and . . .

Toddy and Aloysius, watched from inside the door.

'He said he was gonna show 'em,' Aloysius explained.

'We better get out there,' said Toddy, 'on accounta how the Boss might need . . .'

Toddy was interrupted by screams . . . thumps . . . more screams . . . screams fading into the distance and . . . the Thief came back into the lair.

'Mm,' he said, pouting contentedly. 'I enjoyed that.'

The Thief brushed a few bits of dust from his clothes, and . . .

The scene dissolved again into streaming light. Miz T was tight-lipped as she wished the Book forward in time and then . . .

'Right,' she said. 'We're back where we came in. The present. Let's have a quick look at how your brother's getting on.' Miz T changed her balance, squinted, and . . . Sam and Miz T materialized in the present in the Ink Thief's lair. There was Jim looking red-faced and excited, and the Thief, following behind him, looking even more excited than Jim.

'Are you sure, my dear?' the Thief asked.

'Well, I don't understand all the quantum chemistry of it,' Jim replied, 'but the Book hasn't been wrong yet.'

The Thief followed Jim to the Book of the Ink Thief. Jim touched the page. It was obviously a special moment for him, and the Thief was right with him.

'Gosh,' said Jim, 'if it works we could do . . . anything.'

'Tiggle and the OOB will try to stop us,' the Thief cautioned.

'I don't think they can,' Jim said.

'They still have your sister,' the Thief reminded him.

'Tiggle will be convincing her that the world should be as it is. She is with Tiggle as you are with me, and the time may come when they try to prevent . . .'

'We'll get Sam back,' Jim said. 'She'll understand. She'll see how wonderful the world will be when Man can control it.'

'Man,' the Thief almost sang to himself. 'Control. Short words, but sweet.'

Miz T was disgusted. 'Man indeed,' she said.

'Oh, Jim, you dimbo!' Sam shouted, but this time Jim heard nothing.

The Thief smiled. He looked around. He called out to his helpers: 'Where are my faithful servants? Toddy, Aloysius, come. Your Master is about to attempt a great transformation. Dear Jim has made a discovery.'

Before Sam could find out what Jim's discovery was, the scene swirled and dissolved and . . .

Sam and Miz T were back, in front of the Strange Book, in the parlour. Miz T landed running. She *stood* up out of her chair, *closed* the Book, and beckoned to Sam.

'Come on,' she said. 'No time to waste.'

'What's he . . .?' Sam began.

'I don't know,' said Miz T, cutting her off, 'but I know that brother of yours understands that Book. If he says he's got something that'll let them do *anything*, I reckon he probably does. It's time to call the OOB. Grab that trolley.'

Sam took hold of the book trolley and scooted along with it, keeping up with Miz Tiggle as she shot out into the library. Corridors through the shelves of books radiated away from the central hall. Miz T stopped before one of them. It seemed to go a *long* way back, receding beyond the horizon. Miz T turned to Sam.

'You're about to use the Screwy Decimal System,' she announced. 'Invented in 1885 by me, Lutitia Tiggle. I imagined this dress in the same year. System's been as dependable as the dress. Organizes the imagination. The System, not the dress. Goes right back to the beginning of time. Big job organizing it all, but it had to be done. Only way to have an OOB.'

'You *still* haven't told me what the OOB is,' Sam reminded her.

Miz T reached into a pocket and pulled out several slips of paper. She selected one, and handed it to Sam. 'I'm going to do better than telling,' she said. 'I'm going to show you. Take the trolley down this aisle and get books number .00B1, .00B7, and .00B43–60. The numbers are on the slip. Pay attention to the numbers, and don't be distracted or frightened by anything you see or hear.'

'I'm not a total wimp, y'know,' Sam said. 'I'm not going to get frightened of a corridor in a library.'

'Good,' Miz T replied. 'If you pass through the one in ancient Sumeria, be careful with the clay tablets. They break. Some of the libraries around the sixth century BC can be confusing, and the old one on Mars is decidedly strange . . . Not to worry. Just stick to the numbers and you'll be all right. Get the books and get right back.'

Without further explanation, Miz Tiggle turned and started to walk off.

'Sixth century?' Sam said. 'Mars? What are you *talking* about.'

Miz T paused and looked back. 'It's the Screwy Decimal System,' she said. 'Makes time and space go a bit screwy. Thus the name. Watch the numbers.'

Miz Tiggle walked off, and Sam was left at the start of the seemingly endless aisle. She thought for a moment, shrugged, turned the trolley around and did as she'd been told.

In the Ink Thief's lair the Thief, Jim, Toddy and Aloysius were on their hands and knees on the Thief's desk. It was a silly picture, and Toddy kept getting pushed out of it onto the floor, but it was the only way to read the writing along the binding of the Book.

'What if we threw the whole Book in?' the Thief asked Jim.

'I think it would wipe out the Shop,' Jim said. 'The instructions are very clear. It's only this page.'

'And to think it was there all the time,' the Thief reflected. 'How could I have missed it?'

'Probably because the writing's almost inside the binding,' Jim explained. 'I only noticed it because of the dots of ink.'

The Thief knelt close to the Book and read the words above the line of ink dots: 'Tear along the dotted line.' 'The opposite page gives instructions,' Jim said. 'It will use an awful lot of Power, but it turns the Power into Powers. You'll be able to do the most amazing . . . wait.'

Jim stared at the Book. He listened to it and then . . . very deliberately . . . he moved and his head disappeared, as though he'd stuck it through a window into another dimension . . . only for a moment . . . then he was back. 'It's the OOB,' he said. 'It's meeting to stop us. It's going to use the other Books, the Strange Ones.'

The Thief raised up sharply to his knees, knocking Toddy off balance. Toddy grabbed Aloysius for support, and both of them fell off the desk, and Aloysius gave Toddy a loud thwack with his bone-club and . . . the Thief paid no attention to any of this. He grabbed hold of the page in the Book and ... ripped it out with follow-through and style.

'*Yes!*' he cried. 'Oh, I do love a good climax. The OOB gathers to destroy us, only to find ... Super Thief! Come, Jim ... let's do it! Toddy ... to the Machine!'

Toddy, responding to his Master's voice, followed Jim and the Thief to the Machine. Aloysius, left with nothing much to amuse him, started to read the instructions for using the Special Page of the Book. He looked impressed. Very impressed. 'Ow! Heavy!' he said. 'Super-Power lunch. This I got to see.'

An impossible number of aisles went off into the impossible distance in Miz Tiggle's small library. Was it possible that Sam was coming down all of them at once? Every single aisle seemed to echo with her voice ... doing a strange duet with the barkings and howlings of ... Dog! 'Waaoooooh!' Sam shouted. 'Aroooooooo!' Dog replied. 'Yeeeeeeow!' bellowed Sam. 'Ruf! Ruf! Haaaaar-ruf!' Dog barked. 'Good books! Mush! Mush!'

Sam and Dog faded in to the library, seemingly out of nowhere. Sam was riding on the trolley. Dog was pushing it. They careened across the floor and came to a screeching stop in front of Miz Tiggle.

'I got a little lost,' said Sam, slightly out of breath, 'but I found Dog, and here are the books.' 'Good,' Miz T replied. 'They're the Bored Directors. Can't start without them. Wish I could, sometimes, but there you have it. So ... the nine squillianth and third meeting of the Official Organization of Bumps is hereby called to order.'

'Official Organization of Bumps?' said Sam, looking puzzled.

'That's right,' Miz T said. 'O.O.B. OOB. Them.'

Miz Tiggle pointed, and Sam watched open-mouthed as . . . washes of colour came wafting out of the books on the trolley . . . out of books on the shelves in front of her . . . out of books on the shelves around her . . . and the colour formed into cartoon Bumps who morphed into Bump Bumps. From the trolley came Lorni Snoop, Shake Rattle and Roll, Creaker, Thumper, and Bumps Sam had never seen before: Sir Bumpalot, the Bumpess, the Moonshooters, the Goose Bump . . .

It's a manic gathering, as all the Bumps hit the library in mid-silliness. Bumps are one-track beings. Lorni is the Bump of curiosity. Sir Bumpalot gets bumped. A lot. The Bumpess is Nobility and Caring If Several Sandwiches Short Of A Picnic. The Moonshooters are Shooting For The Moon. (Really. With a pop-gun. It's all a question of figuring out how long the required piece of string is – and maybe a bigger pop-gun.) With each Bump doing its own silly thing for all it's worth, calling this meeting to order seems an impossible undertaking. The floor of the library is very loony and very loud, which makes a calm change from the balcony. Up there Bumps are hanging over the railings, topping each other with silly business, falling asleep, falling over the railings and . . .

Sam and Miz Tiggle stood in the middle of all the noise and chaos. Sam was just slightly gobsmacked. Miz Tiggle was waiting. Finally she reached over to the wall and took down a big sign. It said 'QUIET PLEASE'. Miz T handed the sign to Dog. It seemed that Dog had done this before. She waded out into the crowd, holding up the sign. Sam had to wade in after her to tell her she was holding it upside down. Miz Tiggle waited a bit longer. Then, firmly, she said: 'QUIET please.' The incredible noise continued. Miz T spoke again: '*Quiet please!*' she said, very firmly indeed. The sound level didn't change. '**QUIET PLEASE!!!**' Miz T bellowed. This time her voice flattened most of the Bumps. The volume was phenomenal. Silence descended. 'Thank you,' said Miz T, graciously. 'On behalf of the Bored Directors . . .'

Miz T was interrupted by an incredibly loud snore. Slumped in an armchair, the Bumpess looked grand, noble in a magnificently silly sort of way, and fast asleep. Miz T looked at her sternly, then whispered to Dog, who . . . bounced over to the Bumpess and gave her a big, wet lick on the face.

'Hey? Wazzat?' the Bumpess mumbled as she emerged sharply, if a bit sloppily, into consciousness. She looked around. She saw Miz Tiggle. 'Ah, Lutitia,' she drawled. 'Many thanks on behalf of the Bored. Glad you could come. Wake me if anything exciting happens, won't you?'

'Thank you for sharing that, Bumpess,' Miz Tiggle replied. 'Now, as I was saying, I welcome you all to this Extraordinary General Meeting to deal with a renegade Bump and a great danger to our Organization, to the world, and to himself.'

'And to my brother,' Sam added.

The library stirred with curiosity as the Bumps leaned, stretched, and climbed on each other to get a better look at Sam.

'And to Samantha's brother,' Miz T agreed. 'Finally, and not a moment too soon, we are going to deal with the Ink Thief.'

The Bumps reacted to this news with a minor attack of panic and hysteria and it was chaos in the library and . . .

*

It's chaos around the Ink Thief. He's surrounded by Power containers of every size and description. He looks as though he's been drinking heavily. The air around him also looks as though it's had a few drinks of Power too many. It's filled with sparklings, cracklings and odd disturbances. Toddy slaves over a hot machine. Jim stands near him, the Page from the Book in his hand. Aloysius watches the Thief with interest and the Thief sees him watching and he gurgles: 'You drink I'm thunk on Power? Naah! Not yet . . . but I'm endeavo . . . endevy . . . I'm workin' on it!'

Jim had left Toddy at the machine, and now he was studying the Thief.

'I think he's had enough Power,' Jim told Aloysius. 'Now the Page.'

Aloysius followed as Jim took the special Page off the desk and carried it to the Machine. He watched as Jim placed the Page into the hopper. He watched as Toddy tried to flip Jim into the hopper as well, and his bone-club landed so hard on Toddy's head that the sound of it hurt. Toddy hardly noticed. The important thing now was to run the machine and cook up the Special Page for the Boss. He'd get the nasty, smelly, stinky, horrible kid another time.

Toddy pulled levers, turned wheels, and Jim followed him and Aloysius followed Jim and the Machine shook and smoked and shone with coloured lights and . . . a single drop emerged from the outlet. It wasn't golden . . . it was diamond. It was like a miniature sun. Jim caught it in a glass, and motioned to Toddy and Aloysius. Then, glass in hand, he approached the totally Power-sozzled Thief and . . .

Aloysius pinned the Thief's arms to his side with one arm. With the other hand, he opened the Thief's mouth. Jim poured in the single diamond drop and . . . the Thief began to tremble. The room began to tremble. The Thief steamed. He flamed. He moved his arm . . . and Aloysius was flung away like a rag doll. The pressure built inside the Thief. A wind swirled around him. He spread his arms and the whole lair seemed to expand and twist and . . . the Thief slowly folded his arms and the lair shrank back to normal. It was absolutely silent. The Ink Thief smiled . . . and reached out his hand . . . and Toddy, on the other side of the lair, was lifted off the ground and flung up against the wall with a noise like thunder. Then the Thief laughed, and his laughter was millions of miles the wrong side of out to lunch.

CHAPTER FOUR

Earth, Water, Cheese and Air

In the library, Miz Tiggle had just announced that the Official Organization of Bumps were finally going to deal with the Ink Thief. The Official Organization of Bumps had considered this news for several seconds. Now they were climbing the furniture in panic. 'Deal with the Ink Thief?' Lorni wailed. 'Us? The Ink Thief? WAAAAALH!!!!'

On the balcony, Bumps were climbing the walls and each other in fear, consternation, and general excitement. On the library floor it was much the same, with Bumps rushing for the exits, rushing back to their chairs and getting generally wound up. The only and striking exception to this behaviour was the nearest, seated row of Bumps: the Bored Directors. They looked Bored out of their brains.

Sam couldn't help being amused by all the loony goings on, but she was also disappointed. '*This* is the OOB?' she asked. '*This* is what's going to help save Jim from the Ink Thief?'

'Strange indeed are the workings,' Miz T replied. 'You'll see.'

Miz Tiggle made her way to the centre of the floor, and her voice cut through the noise and probably also the foundations of the building as she said '*SILENCE PLEASE!!!!!!!!!*'

There was silence, except for a few loose bits of masonry

falling and the rustlings and snores of the Bumpess. Miz T indicated the Bumpess to Dog, who galloped over and gave her another sloppy lick.

The Bumpess woke. 'Well, I'm *supposed* to be bored,' she declared. 'We're the Bored Directors. Stands to reason. What's the point of the OOB *having* Bored Directors if we're not? Bored, I mean.'

'Helloise, dear,' said Miz Tiggle, sweetly, 'just stay with us temporarily. We'll need your unusual mental abilities.'

The Bumpess was pleased. 'Ah, well,' she said, 'that's different. I'm hardly ever bored if it's me doing the talking. Dealing with the Ink Thief, are we? Fine. I shall . . . think.'

'Splendid,' Miz T replied, and was about to go on when Sir Bumpalot interrupted. He had finally figured out what was going on.

'A knight doesn't need to think,' he blustered. 'We have here a damsel in distress. Lady, you can count on me.'

Sir B bowed to Sam. He was about to go on when he was interrupted by the Moonshooters. They had been talking animatedly among themselves. Now they addressed the other Bumps: 'Ah . . . Um,' Moonshooter I began. 'My colleague and I have already thinked. P'raps once we get the right length of piece of string, an' the right size of pop-gun . . .'

'An' we HITS the Moon,' Moonshooter 2 continued, 'an' we climbs up the string, then p'raps we can break off some cheese and make a introplanetray cheese projectile, what . . .'

The Bumpess, who seemed to have nodded off again, was suddenly wide awake. 'Cheese?' she exclaimed. 'Of course. Lutitia, why didn't you think of that?' Miz T turned triumphantly to Sam. 'Hah!' she said. 'You see, Samantha? The Official Organization of Bumps may work in mysterious ways, but we always get there in the end.'

'Get where?' Sam asked, losing patience. 'What's cheese got to do with anything? What are you *talking* about?'

'I'm talking,' Miz T declared, 'about an archetypal adventure, a journey of one hundred light centuries, a search, a race against time . . . Where's Dog?'

Dog zipped to Miz Tiggle's side. ''Ere's me, Miz T,' she panted.

'Adventure time,' Miz T announced.

'Yeah,' Dog barked. 'Woo. 'Venture time!'

Leaving the ground with excitement, Dog tore out of the meeting, sending Bumps spinning all over the place.

Cheese was also on the menu in the Ink Thief's lair. The Thief and his servants were watching as Jim studied the glowing Book. He looked concerned as he turned to the Thief. 'At first I thought it was a joke,' he said, 'but searching for it as a variable I found that there *is* actually a multi-dimensional galaxy in which cheese is elemental, and where the structure of an entire satellite is composed of cheese which . . .' The Thief tried to look as though he understood some of this, but he didn't.

'I'm not quite with you, dear boy,' he confessed.

'He's losin' his tooties, boss,' Toddy growled. 'He's got cheese in 'is brains! I know. How 'bout we stick *him* inna Machine an' . . .'

'Cheese?' roared Aloysius, catching up with the conversation. 'Did somebody say cheese?'

Bumps bump off the walls as Dog burns back into the main hall, scattering them and delivering one of the Strange Books to Miz Tiggle. Dog sits and watches carefully as Miz T places the Book on a table and opens it. The buzz of the gathered OOB dies down as Miz T concentrates. Sam is captivated by the sudden silence, broken at last by Miz

Tiggle standing, closing the Strange Book with a satisfied bang, and saying: 'Yes. That should do it. Come.'

Miz Tiggle strides off, followed by an enthusiastic Dog, a puzzled Sam, and a loony OOB. Somehow the crowd of booby Bumps all manage to follow Miz T out the library door and into the dusty corridors. Well, almost all the Bumps follow Miz T . . . all except Lorni. He gets curious. He gets to looking around the corridors. He gets lost.

The rest of the OOB crowded along the corridor, climbing over and under each other, bouncing off the walls and following Miz T as she counted doors. She stopped. She turned a handle, opened a door slowly and there, far far away in infinite starry space, was a spiral galaxy. Sam, pressed forward by the crowd behind her, moved into the doorway to look. She gasped at the sight of the immensity the other side of the door, and gasped again as the crowd behind her almost pushed her through the doorway. If Dog hadn't moved fast, Sam would still be falling.

'Yeow!' Sam breathed. 'Thanks, Dog. I almost fell out there. Where *is* out there? What . . .'

'That's the Aplopalyptic Spiral,' Miz T said. 'It's one hundred light centuries sideways from here and it's where we must go to protect the worlds from the Thief and get James back.'

'Cheese of course,' the Bumpess explained. 'Had to be the Spiral.'

'Could use the pop-gun,' the Moonshooters suggested. 'Everybody could collect string, and . . .'

'Yes,' Miz Tiggle interrupted. 'Well. You two get on with that. Plan B. *We* will go to the Aplopalyptic Spiral. We will find the Four Bumps of the Aplopalypse, who have not been together since the beginning of the Aplopalypse itself. We'll bring them together again. Not even a Selfishness Bump like the Thief can stand against Earth, Water, Cheese and Air. They are the Elemental Bumps. All James's knowledge and science can't help the Thief against the combined power of the Four Bumps of the Aplopalypse.'

The Bumps in the OOB couldn't have been more impressed. 'The Four Bumps, ey? Zowie!' 'Stick *that* in yer ink well, Thief!'

It had to happen. The OOB got excited. Shake Rattle began to boogie. Roll joined in. In seconds the corridor was full of bopping Bumps singing:

> The OOB is up and rockin', everybody
> shake your hips
>
> We're gonna get the Four Bumps from the
> great Aplopalypse
>
> We're gonna go and do it and we never
> will be scared
>
> It doesn't even matter that it's far
> away and weird
>
> Four Bumps, yeay, Four Bumps, oh woah
> woah, Four Bumps, oh yeah
>
> We're gonna get the Four Bumps of the A-
> plop-o-lypse.

'And so say we all,' said Sir Bumpalot.

'Yes,' Miz T sniffed. 'Well. We'll see about that. Anyone who goes to the Aplopalyptic Spiral faces a journey of extreme weirdness. What we are talking about is taking a leap into the unknown from which none of us may return.'

Extreme weirdness? Leap into the unknown? Not return? The OOB went quiet. There was only the shuffling of Bumps trying to slip away without being noticed.

'Ah,' said Sir Bumpalot. 'Slight problem there. Got to stay home in case of dragons.'

'But there aren't any dragons here, you silly man,' said the Bumpess.

'Exactly,' Sir Bumpalot replied.

'Anyhow,' mumbled Thumper, 's'gettin' dark. Gotta go see an attic about a thump.'

'Gotta go see a staircase about a creak,' Creaker added.

As they made their excuses the OOB begin to ease nervously away, keeping their eyes on the dangerously open door to the Aplopalyptic Spiral. The Bumpess was watching her step like all the rest, but she was also watching Miz Tiggle. 'Are you going, Lutitia?' she asked.

''Course I am,' said Miz T. 'This is personal, and you know it.'

'Well,' the Bumpess announced, 'I'm sure the entire OOB joins with me in being behind you all the way, and wishing you a Bumpy ride.'

'All the way,' said Creaker. 'Behind,' said Thumper.

Sam could see that she and Miz Tiggle would be going on, and that the OOB would be staying home.

'Thank you, everybody,' she said. 'I'm sure you've been a big help, I think.'

'Yes,' said Miz T. 'Absolutely. Meeting adjourned.'

The burble of Bumps slipping away down the corridor got brave as they got further away from the door to the Spiral. Sam could just hear them in the distance as they started to sing again:

Earth, Water, Cheese and Air,
you're playing around with fire

When you put them all together, they'll
blow your amplifier

Four Bumps, yeah yeah
Four Bumps, Oh woah woah

We're gonna get the Four Bumps of the
A-plopa-lypse

Sam, Miz T and Dog listened to the fading sound of the
OOB and then heard a bang nearby and . . . Lorni Snoop
stumbled in from a side corridor. 'I got losted,' he said.
'What's happenin'?'

'The Aplopalyptic Spiral,' Miz T replied, as though the
two words were an explanation.

'Oh, right,' said Lorni. 'Oh no! Not the Aplop-op-op —'
Sam cut off Lorni's panic attack. There was a simple
question she needed an answer to. 'Will going there get Jim
back?' she asked Miz Tiggle.

'I'd say it's our only chance,' Miz T answered.

'Then I'm going,' Sam decided. 'I'll go by myself if I
have to.'

'Won't you be scared?' Lorni whispered.

'Sure,' Sam said, 'but I'm going anyhow.' Lorni took a
deep breath. He took Sam's hand.

'Well, then I'm going too,' he said. 'We can be scared
together. I never have anybody to be scared with.'

As the Thief watched, Jim withdrew his head from the
glowing Book of the Thief. He looked worried. Then he
looked in the Book again, looked up, looked dismayed, and
spoke fast.

'The Four Bumps of the Aplopalypse,' he sputtered.
'They're going to a galaxy with a cheese moon to get the
Four Bumps of the Aplopalypse. She's taking Sam with her.

The Book says that together, the Four Bumps are unstopp-
able. They . . .'

The Thief had been looking concerned. Now he smiled
with relief. 'The Four Bumps of the Aplopalypse?' he
laughed. '*That* old act? They haven't been together since
the beginning of Time. Not to worry, my dear.'

'But they've gone to *get* them together!' Jim insisted.
'Sam's gone. How *could* she? How could my own sister
stop us making a perfect world?'

'She can't,' the Thief assured him.

'But the Book says the four Bumps together can neutralize any Power,' Jim continued. 'They're the Elemental
Bumps! What'll we do?'

'Elementally, my dear whatsit,' the Thief replied. 'We
neutralize them first. They're has-beens. Yesterday's Bumps.
History. We follow Tiggle. She finds them, we finish them.
Together they were something . . . once. Not any more.
Earth, Water, Cheese and Air. Terrible name for a group.
Trust me. They have no style. We'll . . .'

'Wait a minute!' a huge voice roared. 'Wait a minute!'

It was Aloysius on the other side of the lair, teaching
Toddy to defend himself. At the moment, Toddy was
hanging upside down from the Rat's fist. Now Aloysius let
go and Toddy got to practise falling on his head as the Rat
scuttled toward Jim and Thief calling out: 'What's all this
about *cheese*?'

Sam and Dog sat at the parlour table, with a Strange Book
open before them. Dog, working hard with her tongue,
seemed to be copying a list from the empty Book. Sam
looked fidgety and bored with book work. 'I think you've
got cats on the brain,' she told Dog.

'RRrr . . .' Dog began to reply, only to be interrupted

by Miz Tiggle bouncing into the room. Bouncing? Absolutely.

'Right,' said Miz T. 'I've changed for the journey. Ready to go?'

Sam looked at Miz Tiggle and looked puzzled. She didn't seem to have changed anything. It wasn't until Dog gleefully pulled up Miz T's skirt and pointed that Sam saw what was changed. Miz T was wearing trainers with her prim Victorian dress . . . trainers exactly like Sam's. Well, almost exactly. Miz T's were grey with a lace trim.

'I liked yours,' Miz T explained. 'Good for a journey. Practical. Prefer my own taste in colours, though. First clothes I've imagined since 1885. Move with the times, I always say.'

A mumbling, grumbling, mop carrying, slop trolley pushing pile of rags works its way down a cobwebbed corridor. It goes to a door, bangs on it and . . .

Toddy went to the door. He peeked through a peephole and . . . the door flew open, smacking him in the head as a filthy, grumbling Thing smashed her trolley into it and entered the lair. Toddy smiled and tried to see the visitor through all the stars and birdies circling around his head. Finally, he focused. 'Oh, it's you,' he said, and danced smilingly over to the Thief, who sat brooding at the big table. 'It's her, Boss,' Toddy announced. His grin widened. His knees gave way. He smiled all the way to the ground, and lay there watching the stars and birdies flying around. The Thief paid no attention to this performance. He peered into the gloom, then recognized who 'her' was.

'Ah, the inferior decorator,' he said. 'And none too soon. *Where have you been, Messa Sloppit?* I told you that tonight was our celebration for Jim and the Dusk of a New Age.

We have special guests. I want finesse. I want flair. I want the place to look awesomely awful, and I want it hours ago.'

'Awwwsomely awwwwwwwwful?' Messa gurgled. 'Allllllright.' Messa Sloppit set mumblingly to work. She slopped nasty puddles from her bucket, just so, rubbed in ugly stains, put up sticky cobwebs, ran gucky stuff down the walls. Jim, watching from the Ink Thief's desk, was fascinated in an awful sort of way.

Under the dining table, Toddy used his fingers to check his head for damage. Satisfied that there was plenty of it, he went to work setting a Gothic-Horrible table for the party. The Thief paid no attention to Toddy, as usual. He was listening to Jim.

'The book says the Awful Allies never come to the same universe twice,' Jim was saying. 'I hope they'll want to stay and help us.'

'Oh, I think they will,' the Thief assured him. 'The Book also says they'll help anyone who has enough Power . . . which I do . . . and I've arranged a really terrible night. They should enjoy it.'

'It's extremely dangerous though,' Jim said, 'inviting them into this dimension. They're very dark forces. Highly entropic. I know it's not a scientific thing to say, but . . . well . . . they're evil.'

The Thief considered this. Evil sounded good to him. Still, he'd have to make it seem all right to the boy. 'Evil,' he said. 'Perhaps, but a necessary evil if the four Bumps *should* get together again.'

'I suppose so,' Jim agreed. 'I guess they're a bit like atomic weapons.'

'Really?' the Thief purred, suddenly fascinated. 'Tell me about atomic weapons.'

*

Dog had written a list. It wasn't a very neat list. In fact, it was a mess. Still, Dog was proud of it. Being a Dog Bump gives one paws when it comes to writing. Dog felt pretty good about the piece of paper Miz T was reading. 'Cataclysm,' Miz T read, 'catacomb, catalectic, catalogue, *catalyst*. Catalyst: Bootlig Bump Alley Cat. Always found in the Wrong Place at the Wrong Time.' Miz T considered. 'That should be easy enough,' she said. 'Little known fact about the Four Bumps. Can only work together if you add a Catalyst to them. No one ever gets the Four Bumps back together because no one bothers about the Catalyst. Told you we could do it. Right. Lorni will catch up with us. Let's go.'

Miz T jumped to her feet. So did Sam. So did Dog. 'Not you,' said Miz Tiggle. 'Sam.'

'Aw Miz T,' Dog whined, 'puhleeese let me go. Puhleeeese let me go. It's a 'venture, an' you *know* I'm good at 'ventures!'

'It's true,' Miz T admitted to Sam. Dog's had adventures even *she* can hardly imagine . . . and this may be her finest hour. Dog is going to protect this end of the universe while we're gone. Dog is going to be our Watchdog.'

'She is?' Dog asked, trembling with excitement. 'I am? Roww! Watchdog, da da da da da da da da Watchdog! Hokay. You go. Dog's gonna watch!'

Messa Sloppit has worked fast. Finished, she spits on the floor, folds her arms, and waits while the Thief inspects the lair. He is *not* pleased.

'Call this atmosphere?' he complains. 'Where's the filth? Where's the decay? Where's the ambience? Would a Phantom live in a place like this? You jest. Would a Dracula? He wouldn't be caught dead in it. It's not good enough.

Tonight is a special occasion, and the place should be *revolting.*' Behind Messa is where you ideally want to be as she spits green spit every place else, grumbles, mumbles, rolls up her sleeves and starts making a really special mess and . . .

Sam went striding down the dusty corridor, keeping up with Miz T. All the doors looked the same, but somehow Miz Tiggle knew exactly which one they wanted. She threw it open and there was the Aplopalyptic Spiral, hanging tiny and distant in star-filled space.

'How do we get there?' Sam asked.

'We jump,' Miz T replied.

'No way,' said Sam.

'I'll jump first,' Miz T offered.

'No.'

'All right, you jump first.'

'No, I said.'

'Why not?'

''Cause I can't fly.'

'Who,' asked Miz Tiggle, 'said anything about flying?'

'What do we do, then?' asked Sam, not at all sure she wanted to hear the answer.

'We fall,' said Miz T.

'But . . .' Sam began.

'Ready?' said Miz T. '1 . . . 2 . . . 3 . . . !'

Seeing that Miz Tiggle was actually jumping, Sam jumped as well.

'Whaaoooooooh!' she yelled as they fell toward the distant Spiral and . . .

'Woaohhhhh!!!' called Lorni, as he fussed and hurried down the corridor and saw them jump and shouted: 'Sam. Miz T. Wait for me!' and . . .

*

A fine scene of gothic horror spreads out before us. Messa Sloppit has given the lair that special, revolting something. Now she dips a ladle into a vat of totally repulsive-looking goo, lifts it out and smells it, adds just a pinch of something, stirs some more, refills the ladle and flings its contents at the wall. Most of the yuck misses the wall and hits Toddy, who accidentally steps in the way. Messa Sloppit considers the whole picture. Mumbling steadily, she goes to Toddy, wipes a single finger-full of yuck off him and flicks it, just *so*, at the pattern on the wall. She's satisfied. The Thief is also satisfied. He sits at the head of the table. Jim sits at his right hand. The table is disgusting. The Thief looks pleased.

The Thief turned to Jim. 'I do believe it's time,' he said. 'The invitations were all received?'

'I checked,' Jim assured him. 'It wasn't very pleasant, but I did. They should come when you call.'

'Doing what a *man* must do is not always pleasant,' said the Thief. Jim considered this.

'I know we need the Awful Allies to be sure we can defeat the Four Bumps,' he said, 'but they *are* horrible. Not a very scientific term is it: horrible? I try to be scientific, but I'm only human, and sometimes it's hard.'

The Thief was offended on behalf of humanity. '*Only* human?' he exclaimed. '*ONLY* human? My dear, dear boy. What is science in aid of if not humanity? Why are you and I down here, away from the world, missing so much, if not for the sake of humanity?'

'Yes,' Jim agreed. 'That's why. I miss my parents and my sister, and I'm afraid of what's coming to dinner, but we *are* here for the sake of humanity.'

The Thief warmed to the thought. 'Humanity,' he said. 'I've given my all for humanity. All my striving, the search for Power, only to leave infinite Bumphood behind and be a winner in the human race . . . and you say you're *only* human.'

By the light of the candles in the unpleasant candelabra, the Thief told Jim the story of his long struggle to stop being Imagination and become a Man. Jim was fascinated. He was moved. He watched the candle flames burning in the Thief's eyes until Toddy walked in and destroyed the mood. With one hand he carried a covered serving tray. With the other he was hitting the yuck seeping out from under the cover, trying to make it stay on the tray. Jim motioned to Toddy for silence. The Thief stood and bowed his head. He looked up. He gestured with both arms and lightning poured from his hands. Thunder rolled. Toddy hid under the table as the empty chairs began to fill with . . . smoke . . . shapes hard to see . . . shapes it would be nicer *not* to see at dinner: the *Awful Allies*. These were *monsters*. Aloysius was a sweet little pet by comparison. The Awful Allies were the worst, the nastiest assortment of Bumps to be found on the Dark Side of the Imagination.

Toddy crept out from under the table. He tried to make himself serve the guests. Then something gooey from a container on his tray oozed out and wrapped itself around his wrist. Toddy was already terrified of who he was serving a meal to. Now the meal was trying to eat *him*. Beating off the appetizers with a serving spoon, Toddy didn't notice as . . .

The Thief raised his glass to his horrible guests. He looked pleased with his little gathering. He looked pale. He staggered. He dropped the glass and Jim rushed to his side. Toddy was too busy hitting the hors-d'oeuvres to see that the Boss was in trouble. The Thief swooned . . . and the Horrible Guests began to fade away. Jim was torn between the Thief's condition and not wanting to lose the Awful

Allies. Holding the Thief, he called out to the fading horrors: 'Wait! Don't go. He'll be all right.'

Jim wasn't exactly sure that the Thief would be all right. In fact, he didn't look all right at all. He looked like a fish out of water as he flapped and faded away.

Suddenly Jim realized what was wrong. 'Power!' he shouted. 'He's running out of Power! Calling the Allies used too much. Toddy! Aloysius! Help!'

Toddy ran to help. He hated the horrible stinky kid, of course, but the Boss was in trouble.

'Hang in dere, Boss,' Toddy moaned. 'Whata we do, kid? Whata we *do*?'

'Start the Machine!' Jim cried. 'Throw in everything we've got. He needs Power.'

'There's nothin' left ta throw,' wailed Toddy. We already throwed it all to make him Super-Boss.'

'All right,' said Jim. 'Stay with him. I'll look in the Book. There must be something we can do.'

Toddy was left fussing over the Boss. He tried to think of something to do. He tried to think of something to say . . . and all he could think of was to sit there worrying and saying, 'Oohh. Nahhh.'

'NAAAAAAAAAAAAAAAAAAAHHHHH!!!!!!!' shrieked Lorni as he held his nose, closed his eyes and jumped through the door to the Aplopalyptic Spiral. In the distance he could see Sam and Miz T falling through the stars. Lorni paddled hard, as though waggling his arms and legs would help him catch up in space. 'Here comes Lorniiiiiiiiiiiiiiiiiii!!!!!!!!!' he screamed.

'Yes! It works!' Jim shouts, and we follow him as he runs back to Toddy and the ghostly Thief. The Thief is fading faster now. You can see right through him.

'Toddy,' says Jim, 'get Aloysius. You've got to move fast.

Here's what we're going to do. Find some Bumps . . . any
Bumps and . . .'

Sam and Miz T fell through space, with Lorni screaming
along behind them and trying to catch up and . . . a planet
floated toward them. Alien continents and oceans grew
bigger and Sam, Miz T and Lorni looked smaller as they
approached the strange world.

The planet looked as big as space itself by the time Lorni
caught up with the others. 'You're supposed to stay *with*
me,' he wailed. 'I'm scared, and we're supposed to be scared
together!'

'How can you be scared, Lorni Snoop?' Miz T
demanded.

'Of course he's scared,' said Sam. 'We're falling into a
planet!'

'Well, aren't you just the least bit curious about what it's
going to be like?' Miz T asked.

'No,' said Sam.

'Oh!' said Lorni.

'It's a whole new world to snoop on,' Miz T pointed
out.

'Golleeeee!' said Lorni.

'Eeeeeeeeeeeeeeeeeeeeee!!!!!!!!' said Sam, as the planet
began to pull the three of them in for a crash-landing.

Jim pulls his face out of the Book of the Ink Thief and runs
across the lair to a low-ceilinged, equipment-filled alcove.
He pushes aside apparatus, pulls down cobweb-covered
dust sheets and reveals . . . a big, old-fashioned knife switch.
It takes all his strength, but he pulls it down and . . . a

circular flap falls open in the low ceiling and . . . a pole pushes up through the floor, up through the hole in the ceiling and stops . . . and makes mechanical noises and . . . returns back into the floor, carrying on top of it . . . the big toy merry-go-round from the toy-shop window. As soon as it's safely on the floor Jim is off, back to the Thief.

The Thief is hardly there at all. Jim puts his hands in his pockets and looks hunched and lost and . . . he feels something. His face lights up and from his pocket he pulls . . . his palmtop computer. Unhesitatingly, he runs to the Power Machine, turns it on, throws levers, turns wheels, and . . . flings his palmtop into the hopper. The Machine gurgles and Jim runs off, returning instantly with a glass which he places below the outlet and waits and . . . Power trickles out into the glass. Half full. Three quarters. Almost full and . . . last . . . drops . . . and . . . Jim rushes the precious Power to the Thief and can just about see where his mouth is and drips power on it and the Thief's mouth moves and his eyes flicker and he starts to swallow the Power and he starts to fade back into substance again but . . . he's still made of pretty thin stuff.

The Thief opened his eyes. 'What's happening, boy?' he whispered.

'We lost the Awful Allies,' said Jim. 'Calling them up used too much Power. You need much more since you got super-powered by the Book but it's okay . . . we're getting more. Lots more. It'll be here soon.'

Sir Bumpalot and Creaker walked together down the corridor. 'I'm only doin' my job,' Creaker squeaked.

'But it's *Bump* armour,' Sir Bumpalot complained. 'Bump armour doesn't have to creak.' Creaker tried to be patient

and explain. 'If you sees a dragon, you gots to try to fight it, right?' he asked.

'Right,' said Sir B. 'Well, if I sees armour, I gots to make it creak.' 'Ah,' said Sir B, 'duty. Quite. A Bump's got to do what a Bump's got to. Stand for something, what?'

Behind the two Bumps there suddenly loomed the giant form of Aloysius and, before Sir B could say 'what', he was inside a dark and smelly sack and deposited on the ground. 'What?!' Sir B finally managed to say. 'WHAT!? Who turned out the lights? How can a fella stand for something lying down?'

Jim ran to Aloysius as the Rat dragged the protesting Sir Bumpalot into the lair. 'Hurry,' he called out. 'Put him in the Machine. We're running out of time.'

'You'll never take Sir Bumpalot,' cried Sir B. 'Ha!'

'Also ha!' said Aloysius as he grabbed the Bump knight and dropped him into the Machine.

'I bumped him off,' Aloysius giggled. 'Nye he he he he.' The Power Machine burbled. It shook. It steamed. It blazed.

'Quick, Toddy!' Jim shouted. 'The buckets!'

Toddy stopped operating the wheels and levers, grabbed buckets, ran for the Power outlet, tripped, juggled and lost the buckets, picked up the buckets and made it to the outlet just as . . . Power came *pouring* out.

'It's working!' Jim cried. 'Aloysius, get the full one. Toddy, bring the rest.'

With Toddy desperately trying to get enough containers under the flow, Jim and Aloysius ran to the Thief. Jim grabbed a soup ladle from the table and ladled Power into the almost invisible Thief's almost invisible mouth. The Thief drank. He shuddered and . . . colour and reality began to return. He stood. He lifted the whole bucket and poured it down his throat. 'That's *better*,' he sighed.

Toddy rushed to his Master with the remaining buckets.

The Thief drank another one. He crackled with Power. He went for the third bucket, stopped, peered into it, and pulled out . . . Sir Bumpalot!? The Bump had been reduced to doll-size. He had a big, foolish grin on his face and . . . he was snoring!

'The machine spitted him out,' said Toddy.

'I set it to leave a little Power in him,' Jim explained. 'He's just sort of hibernating.'

The Thief put the toyed Bump down on the table. 'I admit, dear boy, to being a bit confused,' he said. 'A hibernating Bump, grinning like the idiot he is. An Ink Thief, feeling almost Real, and filled with Power. I am puzzled. Pleased, but puzzled.'

'You needed Power,' said Jim. 'You used too much calling the Awful Allies and you needed lots of it, quickly. I remembered all the Power that came out of Sam's drawing when you put it in the Machine, and I looked for her drawing book but I couldn't find it. Then I had an idea, and I checked it in the Book, and it worked. I thought that if children had more Imagination Power than grown-ups then a Bump, being pure Imagination, must be nothing *but* Power.'

The Thief was stunned. 'So you put a Bump in the Machine,' he said, suddenly understanding. The Thief looked at Jim with admiration. His eyes shone. 'How very human of you,' he purred. 'How wonderful. Where have I been all my life? How could I have missed it? There must be enough Power in all the Bumps in the OOB to make me a Man, defeat the Four Bumps of the Aplopalypse . . .'

'And give mankind a chance to make a perfect world!' Jim concluded happily.

'That too,' the Thief mumbled. 'Yes, Toddy?'

Toddy held up the snoring, smiling, toyed Bump. 'What do I do with this?' he asked.

'Oh, I've got a system for that,' Jim said. 'We're going to have to catch lots of Bumps, so we're going to need a system.'

'Hear that, cat?' Aloysius laughed. 'We're gonna bump off all the Bumps!'

'Yeah!' Toddy agreed. 'Me too! I'm gonna bump 'em and jump 'em and thump 'em an' . . . an' . . . an' . . .'

'A system,' said the Thief, with a mad glint in his eye. 'The dear boy has a system. Aren't humans wonderful?'

The toyed Sir Bumpalot hangs from a hook on the merry-go-round in an alcove of the lair and . . . Jim throws a big switch to start it turning and . . . the Thief, Toddy and Aloysius watch as the merry-go-round turns . . . and rises on its pole . . . into the hole in the ceiling.

As they watched, Jim told the others what he'd found out about the merry-go-round. 'I learned about it from the Book,' he said. 'Some of the earlier Ink Thieves used to actually run the Toy Shop upstairs. They put Imagination Power in toys for children. They used this to send the toys up into the Shop. It's a nice idea. Once we start getting the world right we could do it again.'

Behind Jim's back the Thief made finger-down-the-throat-don't-make-me-sick gestures to Toddy and Aloysius.

'It's a completely, utterly and desperately' – the Thief looked at Jim's well-meaning face and thought quickly – 'sweet idea. But first, we must deal with Tiggle and that bunch of has-beens, the Four Bumps of the Aplopalypse. We've lost the Awful Allies, but I have a feeling that a super-Bump-powered Ink Thief will be all the awful we need. Jim, get ready to travel. Toddy and Aloysius come with me. We're going out to get breakfast.'

In the Toy Shop window, the toyed Sir Bumpalot drops from the turning merry-go-round, bounces over a few toys, and comes to rest in a laid-back position in the toy display. He continues to grin his happy, fixed grin . . . and to snore while . . .

Down below, the Thief stalks the corridors like a vampire. He hears a sound. He smiles. He hides and . . . Thumper comes thumping down the corridor. He *thumps*, 2 . . . 3 . . . 4 and *thumps*, 2 . . . 3 . . . and *thumps*, 2 . . . and *thumps* and stops and looks pleased and hears an extra *thump* . . . and looks puzzled so he *thumps* again and something *thumps* back and he thumps a little rhythm and the rhythm is repeated and it sounds like it's right behind him and he turns very slowly and . . . there is the Ink Thief. The Thief stamps his foot to *thump* one more time and then . . . grabs Thumper and smiles hungrily into the Bump's frightened face. 'Yum,' he drools. 'Breakfast.'

Toddy, too, was stalking the night. Day. Whatever. He heard a sound, hid, and watched as the Goose Bump came waddling down the corridor. Toddy rushed at it. 'Check out the claws,' he hissed as he whipped them out. 'I got style. I got moves. You better not try'n fight me, 'cause I can do things with these that shouldn't happen to a . . .' Toddy felt a tap on the shoulder. He turned slowly and there was . . . 'Dog?!' Toddy wailed.

Dog gave Toddy the special look she reserved for bad cats. Then she stomped on his foot, slapped him over and over under the chin until he was standing nice and straight, took him by the ear and bounced him off a wall. Toddy smiled a crooked, bent-whiskered smile as he danced gently off down the corridor, admiring the nice stars and birdies again.

*

Sam, Miz T and Lorni have also gone from stars to birdies. They've fallen through the Aplopalyptic Spiral galaxy, been watched by strange birds as they dropped noisily through clouds, and have burst into brightness a few hundred feet over a strange, colourful landscape. At the last moment, just as they're about to splat messily all over the place, Miz Tiggle grabs Sam. She shifts like an ice skater and brakes hard with the edges of her feet, screeching them both to a perfect landing on a moss-covered rock.

Lorni splats. He lands flat on his face, spreads out like a raw egg hitting a stone wall . . . then snaps back together again into a wobbling jelly which quietens down into a grinning Lorni Snoop, looking at a whole new world to snoop in. He sees Sam, and tries to tell her how he feels about this. 'Ooooh!' he says.

CHAPTER FIVE

Earth + Water = Muddle

Miz T, Sam and Lorni stood in a jungle of strange and colourful undergrowth. Alien flowering weeds twisted and turned into tunnels and cascades of vegetation over and around them. Then the tangle parted revealing a valley planted with . . . apple cores? Giant apple cores? Lorni was instantly off, with the cry of the Snooping Lorni: 'Ohhhh! Looka! Mmmm.'

Sam was still stunned by their landing on the planet. 'That was incredible!' she said. 'This is incredible. How'd you *do* that? Where are we?'

'Earth . . .' said Miz T. 'How did I do what?'

'That landing. How'd you skate to a landing like that in thin air?'

'Practice,' said Miz T. 'Experience between worlds. It's mostly a question of Mind over It Doesn't Matter. Where on Earth is Lorni?'

'Dunno,' Sam admitted. She couldn't see any sign of him in the alien undergrowth. 'Are you *sure* this is the Earth?' she asked.

'Not *the* Earth.' Miz T replied. '*Earth*, the Element World. Where *is* that Lorni? Full-time job, keeping an eye on Bumps. We'd better get moving. Find the Earth Bump, find the other three and get back to the library. Haven't been away from my Bumps since 1885. I hate to think what they're up to.'

*

Shake Rattle and Roll pop through a dusty wall, boogying. They're followed by a group of all singin', all dancin' Bumps. Shake and the gang float along above the floor, doing their number and . . . Toddy stalks around a corner and Aloysius slides in through one of the doors, with three big sacks slung over his shoulder. Watch out for Aloysius. He's grabbing anyone he can get his paws on and stuffing his sacks full of squealing Bumps.

Toddy pounced, and his sharp claws held Shake Rattle and Roll, and he turned to show Aloysius what he'd caught and . . . the Bumps turned on Toddy. They shook him. They rattled him. They rolled him.

'Keep him reelin' and rockin',' they sang. 'Shake him up, baby, yeah, 'til he's all shook up, hey, hey . . . Hey!?'

A large paw had a grip on Roll's neck. Behind it was Aloysius, who was also the proud owner of a second paw which now held Shake Rattle so tight it made his tongue stick out. Aloysius looked at Toddy and shook his head in despair.

'What's a twinkie, cat?' Aloysius asked.

'A fluffy cake full of squidge?' Toddy said, pretty sure that was the right answer.

'Cat,' said Aloysius, 'you got all the killer instincts of a twinkie. Get the bags.'

Toddy slumped off to where Aloysius had left the three sacks. 'I'm *gonna* be bad,' he promised himself. 'I *am*. I'm gonna *get* Killery Stinks.'

Toddy reached for a sack full of struggling Bumps and . . . a little Bump managed to pop its head through the tied top of the bag. Toddy shoved his face right into the Bump's, and looked as vicious as he could.

'GgggggrooOOOWWW!!' Toddy screeched.

The little Bump's eyes bugged out and it whipped back down into the sack.

Toddy felt better. 'Yeah,' he growled. Killery Stinks!'

Toddy was delighted to find that Aloysius had come for the bags and was watching him. 'Hey! Aloysius!' he shouted. 'Killery Stinks!' Aloysius looked underwhelmed, picked up two sacks full of Bumps, and walked off down the corridor. 'Yer a monster, cat,' he called over his shoulder.

'Yeah,' Toddy agreed. 'I'm a monstener! I got Killery Stinks.'

Full of pride, the Monster Cat grabbed the last sack of Bumps like a kung-fu fighter. 'Ha!' he shouted, and tried to swing the sack up onto his shoulder. Nothing happened. He tried another angle. Better grip. More leverage. He strained until he seemed about to splatter in a messy explosion of cat guts. Nothing. Toddy watched Aloysius walk away carrying two sacks in one hand.

'Aloyyyyy-sius,' he whined. 'Aa-ah-ah.'

Sam leads the way through a riot of colourful, weed-like, complicated and other-worldly vegetation. Miz Tiggle follows behind, lost in thought.

'Things always work out for the best, though,' she tells herself. 'That's how things work.' Despite her words, Miz Tiggle looks worried. Sam, on the other hand, is enjoying this new world. She smells a flower, swings on a vine, does a cartwheel on a flat patch of moss. Miz Tiggle, coming up behind her, can't help smiling. Then she turns a cartwheel of her own. Somehow, this seems to make her feel better.

Lorni snooped into a small clearing. It was like a perfect little garden full of beautiful flowers, and strange butterflies, and . . . a skull looking at him from a wall of stone. It had big teeth and it was smiling at him. Lorni shook . . . then he screamed: 'BlaaAAAAAAAAHHHH!!!!!!!!!!!!. . .' then he ran. He passed Sam before she even realized that it was him. Miz Tiggle saw him coming, though, and caught him as he went past. She dug in her heels and was only dragged a small way before she brought Lorni to a stop. By the time Sam caught up with them Lorni was just about able to talk, and Miz Tiggle's heels were smoking.

'A skele-lele-leleton!' Lorni raved. '*Big* teeth. *Big* mouth! Time to go home. Wrong planet. No Earth here, only monsters . . .'

Beautiful electric guitar chords and a terrific singing voice interrupted Lorni in mid-panic. The music was coming from the direction he'd just left.

'Good music, for a monster,' Sam observed.

'Earthy,' said Miz T.

'Let's have a look,' Sam said. 'Come on, Lorni.'

Miz Tiggle led the way. Sam took Lorni's hand. Lorni took a big, brave breath, and together they set off in the direction of the music and, possibly, the monster.

The Power Machine was red hot from all the Bumps going in and all the Power flowing out. Toddy slaved over a hot Power bucket. He operated the levers, wheels and cogs. He rushed to the outlet and placed fresh containers to catch the Power. He stacked the full ones on a brand-new storage shelf.

Aloysius was enjoying his work. The big Rat was plucking Bumps from a cage and chuckling as he threw them to Toddy. Occasionally he juggled one first, out of pure high spirits. With the Machine full, Aloysius started pulling out the used Bumps whose Power had already been removed. They all had the same goofy smile, they'd all become toys, and each one had its own silly snore. The Rat used his bone-club to bat the toys over the machine to Toddy. 'We apologize for the Bumpy flight . . . nye-he-he-heh!' he chortled. 'Hey cat, heads up. Flight 249 comin' in!' Toddy caught the Bumps, ran them to the merry-go-round, and hung them with all the other toys who were once members of the OOB.

Jim walks along the Machine, watching over the work. He checks dials, counts the bottles on the new Power shelf, and writes down the total with . . . a quill pen and a pot of ink! He hasn't got a computer anymore. His hands ink-stained, his eyes looking lightly poached and his expression troubled, he turns from the machine and sees . . .

The Thief, in a corner of the lair. He's practising the use of the super-powers he gained from the tear-out page of the Book. He drinks a glass of glowing Power, then . . . spins like a gunfighter, pulls out his hand like a gun and . . . a chair whips back and smashes against a wall. He gestures at a surface and . . . it begins to cover itself with noxious ooze. He gestures again, this time putting care, effort and no small amount of spin into it and . . . something ooze-based lifts up out of the general flow of yuck. It develops eyes. Horrible eyes. The mouth which follows makes the eyes look friendly. The Thing looks like it's very happy to have been called into being, so long as it can do terrible things to all the other beings. It laughs a truly awful, gurgling laugh as it subsides back into goo again. The Thief rubs his hands and moves his fingers against his palms, enjoying the crackling power as he asks himself: 'How can anyone be so desperately, evilly, awfully, horribly powerful and altogether superbly *me* as me? Ooh! I'm quite overwhelmed by myself.'

The Thief continued to bubble as Jim, ink-stained and worried, walked into his practice corner. 'Ah Jim, my dear, dear boy,' the Thief drooled. 'You have done wonders. There seems to be no limit to my powers since you had me drink that page from the Book. I knew there were better ways of getting Power from the silly thing than reading it, but this . . . you will be repaid, my boy. We will get your sister back. We'll stop Tiggle. We'll make the Four Bumps of the Aplopalypse wish they'd never gone back on the road and . . . we'll make that better world. The Power is ours!'

'But not enough,' said Jim.

'Not enough what?' the Thief asked.

'Power,' Jim replied. 'We haven't got enough. I've checked my calculations over and over. I've measured flow and storage. Even with all the Power we're getting from the Bumps, it's still not enough to keep you like this *and* make you Real before the Ink Timer runs out. Observing the flow of ink, I'd say we're down to a matter of days before it's all dripped through. Then the Owner comes back, and a new Thief takes over, and . . .'

'*Days?*' the Thief interrupted. 'We don't need days. We strike now. Today. I'm ready. Watch.'

The Thief knocked back another glass of Power and moved his hands like a magician. He pointed across the lair. For a moment nothing seemed to happen and then . . . an enormous cloud boiled out of the wall. It billowed up like a great white shark made out of oil, water and steam. Its mouth was big enough to walk into, and full of rows of sharp and shiny teeth. The Thief snapped his fingers. The monstrosity disappeared.

Jim had been really frightened by the Thing the Thief created, but he still wasn't convinced.

'Yes,' he said, 'we've got the powers to stop the Four

Bumps, but have we got the Power? You're using it almost as fast as I can store it.'

'Trust me, boy,' the Thief replied. 'I'm almost Real. The time is now. We go. We eclipse the Bumps of the Aplopalypse?'

'But the Power deficit . . .' Jim began. 'Trust me,' the Thief repeated.

'But there may not be enough Power to —'

The Thief didn't let Jim finish his sentence. He wrapped his arms around the boy. He tried to be inspiring. 'Jim, Jim . . . a Man doesn't say "can we?" A Man doesn't say "should we?" A Man says . . . that thing you told me . . . goofer it!'

Jim looked puzzled. Then he understood.

'You mean,' he asked, '*go* for it?'

'For your sister,' the Thief enthused. 'For your family. For a perfect world.'

'I could measure out Power rations and try to make it last,' Jim volunteered.

'That's the spirit!' the Thief cried.

'I could ask Aloysius and Toddy to catch Bumps faster.'

'No,' said the Thief, 'I'll ask them. The dear things will do anything if I ask them properly. This is it, my boy. Are you ready?'

'Yes,' said Jim, quietly. He turned from the Thief, then turned back. 'Yes!' he said, and this time he sounded like he meant it. 'It *IS* time. I want to go home to a better world, and I want my sister back, and I want to just go home. Whatever it takes, let's do it!'

Aloysius was asleep. He snoozed in a chair tilted back against the wall. He seemed to be enjoying his dreams. Between snores he snarled and giggled. He had no idea that the Ink Thief was standing nearby, watching him. The Thief pointed his finger and . . . the chair slipped down the wall and Aloysius hit the ground with a serious wake-up thump.

Aloysius got off the floor in kill mode. He didn't stop to look at who he was attacking . . . he just attacked. His eyes opened wide, he showed his ratty teeth and . . . then . . . Aloysius discovered that he couldn't move. The Thief was holding him in strands of what looked like blue lightning.

Now the Thief was moving closer, and closer, and Aloysius was up against the wall and there was nowhere to run even if he *could* run and a silly, frightened grin replaced the 'kill' expression on his face.

'Are you a happy rat, Aloysius?' the Thief asked him.

'Ummmm, yeah,' Aloysius whispered, and tried to shrink away.

'Good life down here?' the Thief wondered. 'Not working too hard?'

'Uh-uh,' said Aloysius, and hoped it was the right answer.

'Think you might work just a teensy bit harder?' asked the Thief.

'Uh-huh,' Aloysius replied, pretty sure he'd got that one right.

'Good,' said the Thief. 'I'm glad . . .'

The Thief moved his hands, and Aloysius was lifted off the ground. In three bounces he was at the Power Machine, with the Thief right next to him.

'I'm very glad,' said the Thief, 'because if you don't work much, *much* harder catching Bumps, the next Bump in the Machine will be you, followed closely by Toddy. You'll tell Toddy, won't you? Good. I told Jim you'd both be *dying* to help, if only I asked you properly.'

Rays of moonlight illuminate the empty library. Walk quietly down the book-lined aisles. The place seems lifeless

without Miz Tiggle. The 'QUIET PLEASE' sign hangs use-
lessly in the silence. Walk on and . . . listen. Whispering
voices. There's a soft glow of light ahead. Move slo-o-owly.
Around the corner. Look.

Dog leaned over the candle, and spoke to the Bumpess.
'Gotta pertek the Liberry,' she said. 'There's notta lotta
Bumps left inna OOB.'

'The Thief and his hench-creatures shall not pass,' the
Bumpess commanded. 'The OOB will protect its Bumps
. . . which brings up certain points of strategiosity.'

'Size of cork,' said the Moonshooters. 'Length of string
. . . Weight of string . . .'

'*Planning*,' said the Bumpess. 'If Lutitia Tiggle were here,
she'd have a plan.'

'Miz Tiggle left me,' Dog proudly reminded them all.
'Watchdog! Watchdog's gonna have a plan. But first . . . I
gotta think.' Dog thought hard. Her eyes crossed, her
tongue waggled and then she said something but you
missed it because . . .

The earthy, smooth, electric guitar music sounds very near
indeed as you look around the garden where Lorni found
the toothy skeleton. Giant red and yellow mushrooms are
dotted around in clumps. In the background there's a wall
of stone.

Sam, Miz T and Lorni peeked around a mass of flowers
into the garden.

'It's beautiful,' Sam sighed.

'Smells good, too,' said Miz T. 'Earthy smells. Earthy
music. If it looks like an Earth world and it smells like an
Earth world and it sounds like an Earth world, I'd say
there's every chance that we've got directly to—'

'The *Monster!*' screamed Lorni. 'AAAAAGGGHH!!!!!!!!'

Sam looked at Miz Tiggle. 'You hold him, Miz T,' she said. 'I'll go look.'

'No-o-o!' Lorni wailed. 'You can't go alone. It's a monster! We gotta come with you an' *protect* you, don't we, Miz Tiggle?'

'Samantha can take care of herself perfectly . . . yes. Quite right! She'll certainly need you to be brave and go with her, won't you Samantha?' said Miz Tiggle.

'I certainly will,' Sam agreed, and winked at Miz T. 'Come on, Lorni.'

Lorni 'protected' Sam as she led the way through the garden. Miz Tiggle followed, watching Sam thoughtfully. They came to the stone wall.

'That's *fabulous*!' Sam said.

Lorni peeked out from between his fingers. 'Not a monster?' he asked.

'Nope.'

'Not gonna eat us?'

'Uh-uh,' Sam said, and leaned against the rock wall. 'It's a fossil. It's a skeleton, in the rock, of something that lived a long time ago. Speaking of rock, it sounds like the music's right . . .'

Sam leaned closer to listen. Her hand touched the fossil and . . . it opened like a door and . . . Sam fell through, and . . . the guitar music stopped and . . . Lorni panicked. 'Ohh, Miz Tiggle!' he wailed. 'Ohh-oh, Miz Tiggle! Sam's fellen inside the skele-lele-lelo . . .'

Miz Tiggle got to Lorni at the same moment that Sam popped back out of the fossil doorway. 'We found him!' Sam called. 'Miz T, we found him! Come on in.'

Inside Rock's house there were more giant mushrooms. They made very comfortable chairs and settees. The creature putting down his guitar and pouring cider for them had the worn, overgrown, eroded look of an old mountain. From the wispy, thinning grasses on his head and the Spanish Moss of his moustache and beard to his stone toes, Rock looked like the Earth element and no fooling.

Having poured cider for his guests, Rock fell heavily back into a large toadstool. 'Oh, yes,' he coughed, 'them was the days. What a combination: Earth, Water, Cheese and Air! You couldn't go anywhere where he wasn't the number one act.'

'What happened to Fire?' asked Sam.

'Didn't last,' Rock replied. 'Terrible hot-head. We did *your* universe with him . . . and it shows. Reality was growin' up. Gettin' mellow. Yer average universe went for Cheese. Sharp, smooth, hard, soft, ol' Cheese had it all. Yes, indeedy, them was the days. Careful with that cider. Brewed in Apple Core Valley. Strong stuff.'

At the back of Rock's cave, Lorni Snoop was admiring the stone discs framed on the walls. 'Each one of them is for a universe we done,' Rock said. 'We musta done . . . oh, dunno *how* many . . . but that was then. The Four Elements are re-*tired*. We sticks to our own worlds now. Don't think we'd remember how to mix it up and shake it any more. Wish I *could* help you folks, but old Rock is back in the Earth world where he belongs. I can't rock 'n' roll like I useta when Things was young.'

'You're not as old as all *that*,' Miz Tiggle sniffed. 'I've been around as long as you, and *I'm* not old at all.'

'It's life on the road, Miz Tiggle,' Rock replied. 'Always another Universe. I got eroded. Water got a little polluted. It happens. Air got blown out, and Cheese . . . Cheese just hangs out in space and stays cool.'

'Please, Rock,' Sam begged, 'you've got to try. We

checked the Strange Books. The Four Bumps can handle any Power. The Four Bumps can stop the Thief. The Four Bumps can get me back my brother. Please don't be old. Please don't be feeble. Miz Tiggle says she's as old as you, and there's nothing feeble about *her*. She's never afraid, and she'll try anything, and she takes care of everybody, and she's brave, and she can run and jump and . . . everything . . . so how can you sit there and say you can't 'cause you're old?'

Rock looked at Miz T. Miz Tiggle looked at Sam and looked embarrassed. 'I know how Rock feels, Sam,' she said. 'I was heading that way myself a bit until you . . . until we . . . well, I know how Rock feels.' Miz T may have known how Rock felt, but now Rock wasn't so sure himself.

'Well, maybe,' he drawled, '. . . just maybe. I do remember a few of the old numbers. I can still do a mean mud-slide, and my quicksand's got a few surprises left. Have to work up to volcanoes, but what the heck. Earth is still stinkin' rich. Maybe there's life in the old Rock yet. Maybe we could get the other three. Maybe we could do it.'

Rock picked up his rock guitar (a truly heavy instrument, half a ton of stone and strings) and began to play and sing:

> Maybe we could rock 'n' roll again.
> Could be that we haven't reached the end.
> Maybe we can do it
> Help to see you through it
> Maybe we could rock 'n' roll again.

Watch out for Lorni. He's wide-eyed at the music. He stands, fills his big chest with air and . . . sings like a rock 'n' roll angel. Possibly even more surprisingly, Miz Tiggle stands and joins him, and she can actually rock 'n' roll. Sam is stunned. Rock does a great guitar solo and everybody shakes, and the cave begins to quake, and the walls begin to break and . . . the music falls apart and Rock's house starts to do likewise.

'W-w-w-what's happening?' asked Sam, bouncing on the moving floor. 'I'm quaking,' Rock screamed. 'Earthquake. I don't *do* earthquakes. Never! I *told* you I was too old to rock 'n' roll again. I gotta lie down and never try to do anything ever again but grow a-a-apple cores in A-a-apple Core V-v-valley and drink the cider and calm my nerves a-a-a-nd . . .'

Lorni crawled on his hands and knees toward the exit, trying to get away. He got to the door. He saw the scenery outside shaking itself to pieces and . . . suddenly Lorni didn't look terrified any more. He looked angry. 'Looka!' he shouted. 'Miz Tiggle, Sam, looka! It's *him*!'

Trees crash, walls smash, and the Ink Thief laughs as he conducts the earthquake like an orchestra. He sees the little figures of Sam and her friends trembling at the entrance to Rock's house. Like a conductor he makes a big, definite move with both arms, and *cuts off* the earthquake in mid-shake. Now everything is horribly quiet, except for a few last loose bits of world crashing down and the Ink Thief's nasty laughter.

In the library, the 'QUIET PLEASE' sign seemed to be working. It was very quiet. Then it was quiet some more. A shadow appeared on one of the big stone pillars. It crept along . . . and there was a loud smash as another shadow smacked the first shadow in the head with the shadow of a bone club and Aloysius said: 'Shhh! Jeez, cat. Do it right, just this once. Now, what are you gonna do?'

'I'm gonna grab books,' shouted Toddy, 'an' *tear* 'em open an *pull* out the Bumps an' *bop* 'em inna brains an' *stick* 'em inna sack until we got ALL OF 'EM!'

'Shhh!!' Aloysius hissed. 'Oh, yeah,' Toddy whispered . . . 'an I'm gonna be reeeel quiet.' ''Cause if you don't . . .?' ''Cause if I don't you're gonna turn me into a cat-burger before the Boss can turn us into toys.'

'Right,' said Aloysius.

'Right,' said Toddy.

The two hench-creatures moved toward the books, then froze at the sound of a voice growling, 'Hello, pussycat.'

'Don' call me a puzzycat,' hissed Toddy. 'Whozat?' They looked around. There was no sign of anyone.

'You go that way,' said Aloysius. 'I'll go this way.'

Toddy nodded. Then he went the same way as Aloysius. Wrong. Aloysius stopped him with a bop on the head and turned him around. Right. They crept off in opposite directions with Toddy still grumbling: ''Cause I'm not a puzzycat' . . . and grabbing handfuls of books off the shelves and growling: 'Puzzycat, huh? Hah!' . . . and throwing the books to the floor, and preparing to grobalize any Bumps inside, and then noticing . . . Dog, standing there watching him.

'Hello, pussycat,' said Dog.

Toddy froze. Then he ran, but Dog was a faster runner.

Aloysius heard all the noise. He started off to investigate. He stopped. There, coming toward him, was the Bumpess. She waved. She beckoned. She disappeared around a corner. Aloysius smiled, hefted his bone club, and followed.

The Ink Thief stood on high ground and looked down on Sam and her friends and laughed and . . . cut off his laughter as sharply as he'd cut off the earthquake. He took a sip of

Power. 'The Four Bumps of the Aplopalypse,' he smirked. 'Seen the act. Terrible. No class. No sense of theatre. Oh the Elements were there all right, but there was no *spark* . . .' On the word 'spark' the Thief reached out a finger and a flash of lightning knocked the watching group flat.

'They never managed,' said the Thief, 'to set the world on *fire!*' As he spat the word 'fire', the Thief went into a complex and unpleasant looking series of movements and Rock looked horrified and screamed 'NO!!!' as he watched the Thief create a living, blazing fire creature. The Thief moved the walking flames like a puppet and sent it burning through Rock's world, spreading toward Sam and her friends. Miz T watched it coming and knew exactly what to do about it.

'Run!' she said. No one argued. They ran, with the fire creature blazing along behind and the Thief shouting, 'You can't outrun it. You don't have the Power.' Jim stood with the Thief and watched. He didn't look happy.

Sam, Miz Tiggle, Lorni and Rock ran for their lives.

'I'll landslide 'im,' Rock rumbled as they ran. 'I'll pulverize 'im. I'll bury that Bump, see if I don't. We'll get the old gang. Come on. Water first. Follow me.'

Sam looked back into the smoke. 'It's catching us!' she shouted.

'Keep running,' Rock called. 'Water'll stop it.'

'There it is,' Miz T said.

'There what is?' Sam panted.

'Edge of the Earth world,' said Miz T.

They were, in fact, coming to an edge beyond which there seemed to be . . . nothing but stars.

'Not again,' Sam moaned.

'Fraid so,' said Miz T, and leapt off into space. Sam followed. Rock got to the edge and wasn't so sure. It was *his* world the Thief was burning down, and maybe he should stay, and . . . Lorni was looking over his shoulder as he made it to the edge and didn't see Rock and ran right into him and Rock fell off his world and Lorni looked down and couldn't jump and the fire creature caught him and . . . the creature burnt out and disappeared with a quiet 'pop'. Only its last spark touched Lorni, but it was enough to make him jump and, once again, Lorni followed the others into galactic space.

Meanwhile, back on the Earth world, the Thief was looking at his hands. They didn't seem to be working. The lightning had stopped streaming from his fingers. The fire creature had vanished.

'What happened to my special effect?' he asked.

'It burnt out,' Jim said. 'You're running low on Power. We have to go back for more. I . . . I . . . I didn't like what happened there.' 'It's nothing,' the Thief assured him. 'They got one of the Four. It doesn't matter if they get two, or three. They need all Four.' 'I don't mean that,' said Jim, sounding angry and upset. 'I mean sending fire after Sam. She could have been hurt. She could have been killed.' The Thief appeared to be shocked. 'Oh my boy, my boy, my boy,' he said, 'how could you even *think* such a thing of me, after all this time? Give me your handkerchief.'

Puzzled, Jim pulled out a crumpled square of cloth and handed it to the Thief.

'I've got a last drop of Power here,' the Thief said. 'Watch.'

From his coat, the Thief pulled out a small vial of Power, drank it and . . . cartoon fire poured from his hand all other the cloth. The handkerchief didn't burn. The flame went out.

'Bump fire, dear boy,' the Thief explained. 'It can't burn real things like handkerchiefs and sisters. It's all right. Don't apologize. Just try to trust me.'

'Yes,' Jim said. 'I was being foolish. I'm sorry.'

'Never mind,' said the Thief. 'I forgive you.' Putting his arm around Jim's shoulders, the Thief led him away. Jim didn't see him point a finger back toward the handkerchief. He didn't see the real flame shooting from the Ink Thief's hand and burning the cloth to white ashes.

Watch out as Toddy knocks over the bookshelves, running for his life through the library with Dog closing on him and . . .

Watch the Bumpess running for all she's worth with Aloysius close behind her and . . .

Look out as Toddy scrambles over the reading table chased by Dog and then Aloysius stomps over it in the other direction, closing in on the Bumpess and . . .

The Bumpess was cornered. Aloysius slid toward her, Bump-bag ready. For some reason, the Bumpess didn't seem to be frightened. 'As Bumpess,' she commanded, 'and in the name of the entire Official Organization of Bumps, I order you to leave this library, you horrid rodent.'

Aloysius was amused. 'Sure,' he said. 'No problem,' he said. 'We'll all go together. You, me, and the entire Official Organization of Bumps. Just deposit yer poopside in this bag, yer Bumpessness.' 'Right,' said the Bumpess. 'You have been warned. Goblin Moonshooters, advance.'

From around a corner the Moonshooters appeared, rolling a *big* pop-gun. It was the size of a cannon, with a cork big enough to knock an elephant over. The Bumpess stepped in front of it, placing herself bravely between the Moonshooters and Aloysius. 'There were Official Bumps before the Ink Thief,' she said, 'and there will be Official Bumps when he is gone. You may surrender now, or the Moonshooters will shoot.'

'No they won't,' said Aloysius.

'They will.'

'They won't. Go on, boys,' said Aloysius, 'Shoot.'

'We can't,' the Moonshooters squeaked.

'Why not?' the Bumpess demanded.

'Technical problem.'

'Oh, for goodness sake,' said the Bumpess. 'What's wrong?'

'You're standing in the way,' said the Moonshooters.

'Ah,' said the Bumpess.

Dog's teeth snap together and there's a little less tip to Toddy's tail as he runs from the library and into the corridors and straight into a wall and . . . Dog corners him. 'Watchdog! da da da da – da da da da Watchdog!'

Toddy flicks out his claws, growls like a cornered cat, strikes . . . and is totally humiliated. Dog puts so many moves on him that Toddy manages to beat himself up trying to hit her. Finally he can take no more and he cries out with all that's left of his lung power: 'Aloyyyyyyyysius!' At the sound of the Rat's name, Dog remembers: 'Oh rats. The Rat. I forgetted the Rat! Don' move, cat. Lie down. Roll over. Stay. Stay.' Dog belts off back to the library. Toddy stays . . . then thinks about what he's doing . . . then tries moving and flinches . . . and nothing happens . . . and he sneaks carefully away and . . .

Aloysius's sack lay on a library floor covered with torn and open books. It bulged, it moved, and from inside it came voices.

"Why didn't you shoot as soon as you saw him?' the Bumpess' voice asked.

'String too short,' a Moonshooter voice replied.

'Well, then, why didn't you shoot when he came right up to you?' demanded the Bumpess.

'String too long.'

Aloysius smiled as he tied up two more wiggling sacks full of Bumps. He plucked a last, stray Bump from its book, threw it in a bag, and walked off laughing his big, horrible laugh and . . .

Dog charged back in to save the library, shouting, 'Watchdog! Da da da da – da da aaAAAAAA!!!! Hada-books! Hada-Bumps! Ha-da-da-da-da-da-da- dumb – dumb Dog! Oh-oh-oh Miz Tiggeelllll . . .' Dog looked at the mess of torn and empty books in despair, raised her head to the ceiling and howled.

There was howling in space as well. Also screaming, as four shapes dropped through a spiral galaxy, and into a solar system, and onto a blue planet. There was a giant *splash*, and Sam found herself underwater, surrounded by strange fish . . . and what she later learned was a pentapus (like a five-legged octopus) and seaweed . . . and a shark coming toward her . . . wearing sunglasses.

'Oh dear, oh dear, oh dear,' Lorni wailed. 'Itsa *shark*! Everybody get behind me on accounta I'm big an' it'll take him a LONG time to eat me an' you can get away!'

'Why Lorni Snoop', said Miz Tiggle. 'You're getting really brave.'

'Uh-uh, Miz Tiggle,' Lorni whined. 'I'm really *s-s-scared*, only . . . Sam's my best friend and you're my other best friend and what's friends for . . .'

'I'd say friends is for lunch the way you amateurs are carryin' on,' said Rock. 'This is business. The shark is Water's agent. Leave it to me.'

Rock rolled over to the shark. They talked fast. A contract appeared. They did a complicated handshake, and Rock returned to the others. 'Okay,' he said. 'We can talk to Water, but if she helps save any universes the shark gets ten per cent. So, Wet Thing,' Rock said to no one Sam could see. 'What about it? We're gettin' the Four Bumps back together. Special charity gig.'

To Sam's surprise, a passing fish answered.

'Rock, you hunk,' the fish bubbled, 'you know I love you, but . . .'

Now a lobster was talking. . . . I'm staying right here. I'm happy. I'm not drained any more. I'm . . .'

'. . . full of life,' said an eel. 'I'd be . . .'

'. . . mad to go on the road again,' the fish said.

'Rock, stop wasting time on them,' Sam complained. 'Talk to Water. Tell her . . .'

'He *is* talking to Water, person thingie,' the lobster said. 'All the water Bumps are Water. You've got eyes and hands and a mouth and things. I've got Fish Bumps and Lobster Bumps and things.'

'All right,' said Miz Tiggle. 'That's enough of that. You can slosh around being talking seafood now, my dear, but it's going to be you or the Ink Thief soon enough, so if I were you I'd want to be the Four Bumps again mighty quick.'

'And what has this Ink Thief got to do with me?' the fish asked.

'He's an awful Bump,' said Sam, 'and he's got my brother and he burnt the Earth world and he knows that only The Four Bumps can stop him and he's stealing Power and if he gets enough he'll be Real and he'll be the worst person ever and . . .'

'Oh, I don't know,' said the Ink Thief's voice. 'Maybe I'll spend my time doing nice, quiet things, like fishing!' The

Thief looked down at them through the surface of the water. Only when he was sure he had everyone's attention did he begin to move his hands and pull everything toward the surface. The lobster, the fish, the pentapus, the eel, all the Water Bumps were pulled toward him and . . .

Water Bumps come flapping out of the water and are . . . netted by Jim, who bags them and nets more and then Jim is thrown aside as a huge wave lifts off the planet. The wave becomes a swirling thunderstorm, the thunderstorm forms into the face of a very pretty and *very* angry woman and . . . Sam, Miz Tiggle, Rock and Lorni ride wildly on top of the Storm.

In his lair the Thief sat at his dining table, enjoying fruit, cheese and a large flagon of Power. He admired a big cage near the machine, filled with miserable looking Bumps. The Thief lifted his flagon to them and drank. Jim watched. He didn't look much happier than the Bumps in the cage.

'Haven't the lads done well?' the Thief slurped. 'Lots of Bumps. Lots of Power. Cheer up, Jim. It was a small set-back.'

'I should have thought of it,' said Jim. 'Of course Water can travel as a storm. I was sure it had to stay on its own planet.'

'Never mind,' said the Thief. 'Cheese doesn't stand a chance. I promise. It will all be over in a day or two and you'll go home a scientific hero.'

'With Sam,' Jim said.

'Safe and sound,' the Thief agreed, and stared at a forkful of cheese until it bubbled and melted.

CHAPTER SIX

Cheese and Ballooney

Aloysius takes his ease in the Ink Thief's lair, lounging in his chair and gnawing on a bone. He stretches. He stands. 'Okay,' he says. 'A Rat's woik is never done. It's a rat-race, is what it is. Fun, fun, fun.' Putting on work gloves the Rat goes to the cage near the Power Machine. The captured Bumps behind the bars cower away as he reaches in and grabs Roll's leg. Shake Rattle won't let Roll go. He grabs the Bump's arms and tries to pull him back into the cage. Aloysius pulls the other way, and poor Roll is stre-e-e-e-etched, and the other Bumps come to Shake Rattle's aid and grab onto Roll and he's stre-e-e-e-e-e-e-e-e-e-e-e-e-e-e-etched some more and Shake Rattle and the others can hold on no longer and Roll *snaps* into a ball and flies out of Aloysius' hands and bounces off a wall and rolls across the Lair with Aloysius following.

'Roll, Roll,' Shake Rattle shouted. 'Roll!' Roll did his best to live up to his name, but Aloysius had all the moves. He caught Roll with his foot and sang 'The Blue Danube Waltz' . . . 'Da da da – da – da – Da, da da, da da, dum de yum dum dum dum, de dum, de dum. . . .' as he . . . flicked Roll up in the air like a football, tapped him with a light header, bounced him off his chest, hit him back up with the outside of his foot, kicked him high up the other way with the outside of his other foot, did some silly ballet while watching Roll descend, caught him with a kick and scored a neat goal in the centre of the Power Machine's hopper.

The merry-go-round rose up from the lair into the Toy

Shop window. It dumped Roll into a jumble of grinning, snoring, toyed Bumps. It looked as though most of the Bumps in the OOB were now sitting in the gloom of the cobwebbed toy display. A flash of lightning played flickering shadows over the toyed Bumps. There was a roll of thunder and a second, white-out flash, and then darkness.

DARKNESS. Thunder rumbles and . . . lightning reveals a jumbled landscape under cloud. As we watch, the cloud clears. The scene becomes lighter, and now we can see that the entire landscape is made of . . . cheeses?

A wall of Swiss cheese glows damply in the dawn light and . . . a small group of travellers appears, walking in front of it. The first to pass is Storm, the Water Bump. She's wild, wet and angry . . . still thundering a bit and flashing the occasional bolt of lightning. Lorni is next. He can't help himself. He's wandering off to snoop. Sam, Miz Tiggle and Rock trail behind.

'Water always travelled as Storm,' Rock said. 'The Four Bumps was a high-powered group, y'know. Heavy elements. Well, this is it. The Big Cheese.'

'A whole Moon made out of cheese,' said Sam. 'It's crazy.'

'So's Cheesey,' Rock said.

'When I first met her she was called Milk. Sweet kid. Too much life on the road turned her.'

'That was then,' Miz T. snapped. 'This is now, and I wouldn't count on the future if we don't hurry up. Where do we find her?'

'She'll find us,' said Rock. 'Cheesey *really* doesn't like findin' things walkin' around on her cheesescape.'

A Strange Book is pulled from its shelf by a paw and Dog flops down at Miz Tiggle's table with it. Dog is not big on concentration, and the effort required shows in her face. She strains. She steers her imagination with her tongue. 'Find Miz Tiggle,' she barks. 'Find. Good Book. No! Not meaty bones. Not cats. No! Bad Book. Miz Tiggle. Yes. Good Book. Good Book!' Dog shuts the Book, turns, gets her legs moving, runs straight at the closed door and straight through it and . . .

Dog tore down the corridor, stopped, counted on her fingers, counted on her toes, counted doors, revved up her legs again to running speed, ran through the closed door she'd chosen and . . . Dog's legs kept moving as she looked down, discovered nothing under her feet, and fell howling toward the Aplopalyptic Spiral.

Rock looked puzzled. Miz T looked irritated. Sam looked around at the cheesescape with continuing fascination and disbelief.

'I just don' understand it,' Rock said. 'Here we are, tromping all over the cheesescape. Cheesey *hates* things tromping on the cheesescape, and when Cheesey hates something she gets really hard about it. Strong. Sharp. She lets you know she's there.'

'Well, she isn't,' said Miz T. 'I mean there. I mean here. Frathersnaggits! You know what I mean. I've got a library full of all the Imagination in a Universe back home. Do you have any idea what all that Imagination could get up to without me and the Screwy Decimal System?'

Sam looked surprised. 'Miz Tiggle', she asked, '. . . are you . . . worried?'

'Certainly not,' said Miz T. 'Things always work out. That's what things do. Only there's a mad Ink Thief in the Toy Shop, and Dog's alone, and . . .'

Miz T was interrupted by a rumble of thunder and a shadow falling over the group and . . . Storm joined the party. The thunder cloud over her head flashed with lightning. 'Where *is* that cheap chunk of cheese?' she stormed. 'I mean yes, I'm the Water Bump. Yes, I'm the flow things are supposed to go with . . . but, right now, I'm Storm and I want action. That Thief took all my little creature Bumps, and when I find him I'm gonna break on him, and when I break on him he's goin' to know he's been broken on! Now let's find that lump of chintzy cheese and let's blow.'

Storm thundered again, just for effect. The thunder was pretty loud, but Lorni's distant screams were even louder. 'Help!' he cried. 'He-e-e-lp! He-buphhhlllll . . .'

Lorni exploded onto the cheesescape, his face covered in white goo. He tried to speak, had to stop to wipe goo off his mouth, then spoke as fast as he could. 'I been goo-ed!', he howled. 'I been goo-ed! I snooped in the cheese and there she was and I said "hello" and she goo-ed me!'

'Looks like Cheesey's found us,' said Rock. 'What's the goo taste like?'

Lorni wiped a bit off with his finger and tasted it. 'Cream cheese,' he said.

'She's found us,' said Rock.

'Right,' Miz Tiggle began, 'where is . . .'

A blob of cream cheese hit Miz T in the face, cutting short her sentence.

'Hmpf,' said Storm. 'Typical.' Storm showered the goo off Miz Tiggle, who was left wet and furious. She looked around, steaming. Her eyes widened. She ducked and . . . another wodge of cream cheese hit Sam in the face and . . .

A figure emerged from a hole in the Emmental. Cheese was made of, well, cheese. She could be sweet and mild when she wanted to. Right now she didn't want to. She reached into one of the holes in the Emmental and started to fling handfuls of cream cheese, while shouting at the travellers: 'Hey! You! Get off of my cheesescape! I'm losing my cool, and if I go on losing my cool I'm gonna get rancid and when I get rancid I'm fierce!'

Miz Tiggle, Rock, Lorni, and a mostly cleaned but wet Sam hid behind a lump of hard cheese and Storm stood out in the open, flashing and thundering. 'Listen, you hunk of dribble from the Cosmic Cow,' she roared, 'we're gettin' the Four Bumps back on the road and we're gonna save a universe and stop a Thief and get my Water Bumps back . . . so wiggle that mouldy pile of muck you use for a body over here and let's go!'

Cheesey considered this, and Sam and her friends considered Cheesey . . . and Cheesey reached into another hole in the Emmental and started throwing balls of crumbly cheese. Sam looked sick. Miz Tiggle went green.

'Uck!' Sam gagged. 'What's that *smell*?'

'She's throwin' smelly cheese,' said Miz Tiggle, 'and I'm havin' no more of it.'

Miz Tiggle charged toward Cheesey. The others followed. Cheesey retreated into the Emmental and defended it by throwing all kinds of cheese at them from the different openings: hard cheese, soft cheese, smelly cheese, and a thin wedge of cheese which chopped a piece out of Rock's hair.

'Doo-eee!' Rock commented. 'That was close. She's throwin' the sharp cheese.'

Storm raged. This wasn't really all that helpful. It meant that Cheesey wouldn't see where to throw, but the others couldn't see where to go and everyone started slipping and falling on the wet cheesescape and . . .

Dog slipped through space, whizzed through black holes, screeched around a star, tumbled out of control toward a planet, missed it, and fell straight into a strange, yellowish moon while . . . Sam and her friends struggled in the wet and storm toward the Emmental and Cheesey peered out to try to see where to throw next and Dog's voice came screaming through the sky: 'aaaaaahhhhhh-AAAAAAHHHHHHHHHHHHHH!!!!!!!!!!!!'

Dog's fall was broken by hitting Cheesey as she leaned out of the Emmental. Now Dog lay on top of a very still Cheesey. Storm turned into a light shower, then her weather cleared. Dog was off Cheesey with a bounce, and all over Sam and Miz Tiggle and Lorni. Storm and Rock bent over the fallen Cheesey. 'Cheesey,' moaned Storm. 'Cheese, sweetie, speak to me.'

'Jee,' said Rock, 'I hope she's all right. I mean Cheese is what made the Four Bumps original. She was the funny element. I mean we're just like all the rest without Cheese.'

Without opening her eyes, Cheesey spoke. 'You really think so?' she said. Cheesey opened her eyes. She sat up. 'Wait 'til you see how good I am now that I've aged a little,' she crooned.

Dog couldn't quite calm down enough to speak. Finally, with Sam's help, she managed to get some words out. 'An' I was Watchdog,' she panted, 'so I had to stay and then I scared the cat and then there was books *a-a-a-a-a-ll* onna ground and ooohhhh Miz Tiggle *come* back Miz Tiggle *come*, good Miz Tiggle 'cause . . . he's got parcally ALL the Bumps inna *whole* OOB an . . .'

'Who's got all the Bumps?' Miz Tiggle interrupted.

'He does.'

'*Who* does?' Sam repeated.

'I do,' said a voice.

There, on a Camembert, stood the Ink Thief. He took a container of Power out of his cloak and poured it into his mouth as Miz Tiggle came striding toward him. Sam was right next to her, matching Miz Tiggle stride for stride. 'What have you done with my Bumps, you, you . . .' Miz Tiggle began.

'Creep!' said Sam, finishing the sentence for her.

'*What*, creep?!' Miz Tiggle shouted.

'Oh, don't worry,' the Ink Thief purred. 'They're all smiles. We're really very close now, the Bumps in the OOB and I. Speaking of close, I think you've got close enough.' The Thief grinned a twisted mocking grin and his eyes begin to glow, and . . . the cheese under Sam and Miz T melted in the heat from his eyes. Their feet sank in the goo and . . . the Thief focused the heat on Cheesey. 'Oh dear,' he said, 'it looks like you can forget about getting the Four Bumps back together. I'm afraid Cheese is going soft on you. Let's face it, friends, she's no longer cool.'

With one bound Miz Tiggle was out of the melting cheese. She stood between the Thief and Cheesey, taking the heat. The Thief poured it on, harder and hotter waves of flame and . . . Sam couldn't believe it. The flames bounced off Miz T! They couldn't touch her. Now she was walking straight for the Thief. He threw heat. She threw it back. He threw lightning. She laughed at it. He threw . . . The Thief's hands were sputtering. He had nothing left to throw, and still Miz Tiggle was coming, looking like the hero in a Kung-Fu Librarian movie. High kicks and all.

'Fratherinsnaggits!' cried the Thief as he turned and ran.

The cheesescape had hardened up again. Dog could run on it. It seemed that she might just catch the Ink Thief as they disappeared behind a hill of cheddar.

'It's Something to do With Dimensions,' was how Miz T explained her surprising powers to Sam. She also said that it was very important never to use them. Well, hardly ever. Rock was amazed. 'He just gave up,' the big boulder said with admiration.

'He hasn't given up,' said Miz T. 'Hurry now. We've got to find the Fourth Bump and the Catalyst and get after him. Dog said he's done something to the Library and the Bumps, and . . . where is Dog?'

'Dog?' Sam called. 'Dog! Dog?!!?!'

Messa Sloppit looks down the length of a derelict, cobwebbed corridor. She shakes her head, mumbles in disgust and sets to work. We watch as she and her cart roll toward us, yuck and hard work doing to the corridor what centuries of neglect could never hope to match. As close to us as she can get, Messa takes a spoonful of steaming and revolting slop, aims it straight at us, adjusts for spin and throw-weight, goes for the throw and . . . stops at the sound of a door slamming. Grumbling mightily, she plops the spoon in the yuck bucket and wheels past us out of frame.

The corridor festers quietly until . . . the cobwebbed silence is broken by a door being thrown open and Dog skidding through it, her legs flying in all directions as she corners hard and disappears through a second door. Through the first door comes the Ink Thief howling with fury and just in time to spot Dog and chase her through the second door and . . . Dog bursts out of a third door while the Thief comes crashing through a fourth door and they're going so fast they pass each other in the corridor and Dog runs through door five and the Thief goes through door one and runs back into the corridor through door two and he's looking a bit puffed and he stops, and he turns, and he walks back through door two and disappears and Dog quietly opens door five and tiptoes over to door two and gently closes and locks it with the Thief inside it and sneaks away through door six too exhausted and relieved to look where she's going but we see what's on the other side of the door and we'd call out to Dog if we could because on the other side of door six is . . .

Dog leaned against the inside of the door, panting. She

wiped the sweat from her eyes with her paw. She sighed. She looked up and . . . the Ink Thief smiled. Toddy waved. Dog turned to run, but Aloysius' big hand slammed into the door, holding it tightly closed.

Aloysius and Toddy dragged Dog past Jim. He looked frazzled, exhausted, wild eyed. The Thief was watching him as he worked hard with the quantum chemical apparatus and the Book of the Thief. 'Having powers takes so much Power,' Jim said. 'There's nothing left to make you Real. It's got to be one or the other.'

'No,' said the Thief. 'I have to have it all. The defeat of the enemy. The Power to be Something and to change the world of things . . .'

'For good,' said Jim, a spark of life returning to his face. 'For happiness. For a perfect world.'

'Absolutely,' the Thief said. 'To change things . . . for good. It will be perfect, Jim, but we must find Power faster. It ran out. Against Tiggle. It was . . . humiliating. I must have more Power. I must stop Tiggle getting the Fourth Bump of the Aplopalypse.'

Jim was exhausted. 'I'm doing my best,' he said, 'only I'm tired and I can't seem to think properly. The Bumps in the cage might be just enough. We'd be safer with a few more.' The Thief was delighted. 'Just a few more? Good. Wonderful. Why didn't you say so? Toddy. Aloysius. Come to me!'

Toddy lay on top of the Bump cage. Inside, Dog looked miserable and forlorn. 'Yeah,' Toddy teased, 'an' then I'm gonna get you outa the cage, an' I'm gonna pull yer ears . . . an' I'm gonna *twist* yer nose and *then* I'm gonna put you inna Machine an' get all the Power outa you an' then I'm gonna stick you in the Toy Shop window on sale *cheap*. Hah! An then . . .'

Toddy's fun was interrupted by the Ink Thief's voice, loud and not pleased. 'Toddy! Now!!'

'Gotta go be a bad cat,' said Toddy, 'but I'll be back!' He

trundled off, trying to look bad, and Dog was left drooping in the cage. 'Some Watchdog,' she growled. 'Pfooey!'

Behind a closed door, a brightness grows. As it increases in brilliance, sheets of light pour into the dim, dusty corridor from the gaps between door and frame. The light steadies, begins to dim and . . . the door opens. There, light spilling all around them, are four figures. They walk through the doorway. The light fades and we see that the four are Lorni, Rock, Storm, and Cheesey.

At the door to the lair, the Thief discussed strategy with his hench-creatures. 'A few more Bumps could make all the difference, so off you go boys . . . and find those last few Bumps, because if you don't . . . I know a certain two I could get my hand on . . . right away.'

'Oh, well we'll get those two for you, Boss,' said Toddy. 'Where are they?'

Aloysius sighed, took a confused Toddy by the scruff of the neck and half-walked, half-carried him off to go Bump hunting.

'I don't get it,' Toddy was saying as they went through the door. 'Why doesn't anyone ever *explain* anything to me?'

Sam and Miz Tiggle descended through a cloudscape of pinks, yellows and blues. Only the wind flapping their clothes and hair gave a sense of the speed with which they were dropping. Unlike previous falls, though, this one didn't seem to frighten Sam at all.

'Always my favourite world in the Spiral!' Miz Tiggle shouted over the sound of rushing wind. ''Specially this time of day. There's nothing like an Airy dawn. 'Course I haven't seen the place in centuries, and I never have met yer actual Air Bump itself . . .'

'We'll find it,' said Sam, confidently. 'We're so much quicker and sharper when it's just the two of us.'

'Good thing, too,' Miz T said, 'things being as they are. Right. Here it comes. Ready to land? Feet together, turn 'em sideways and . . .' Miz T watched as Sam did a perfect ice-skater's stop, landing softly on a swirling, cloudy surface.

'Good,' said Miz T. 'You're learning.'

Lorni led three Bumps from the Four Bumps of the Aplopalypse into the main room of the Library and . . . stopped, horrified at what he saw. The place was a mess. There were books lying torn and empty all over the floor.

'Dog?' Lorni called. 'Do-o-og? DOG!!' Lorni was frightened for a moment by the echo of his own shout. Then he ran to the books still on the shelves and started knocking on their spines.

'Hello?' he said. 'Anybody home? Open up. Come out! Where is everybody? OHhhhhhhh . . . gone?'

Lorni ran back to the Three Bumps in despair. 'They're all gone!' he wailed. 'Not a Bump in a book. Not a book with a Bump! No Dog. Ohhh . . . big trouble. He's tooken all the Bumps! What're we gonna do? What're we gonna . . .'

The front door to the library slammed shut. Someone was coming. Lorni motioned to the Three Bumps for silence, tiptoed away to see who it was .·. . and tiptoed back, terrified. 'It's them,' he squeaked. 'It's they. It's the Cat and the Rat. I gotta hide you. If they find you, Ohhhh deah, what'm I gonna . . .'

Storm couldn't believe Lorni's wimpy attitude. 'Come on, Snoop,' she said. 'Stop being such a drip. You know, you'd be really cute if you dried up.'

'I don' have *time* to be cute,' Lorni howled. 'I gotta hide you! Fast!'

'Well, it's a Bump library,' Cheesey pointed out.

'Strange Books?'

'In the parlour,' said Lorni. 'What are we gonna . . . yeah! Strange Books!'

Beaming with sudden hope, Lorni led the others to the parlour, closed the door behind them, and leaned against it as Toddy and Aloysius come into view. The Rat and the Cat were surprised and delighted.

'Hey cat,' Aloysius rumbled. 'Look. I think it's the Chicken Bump, nye-he-he-he-he-he.' 'Nye-he-he-he-he,' Toddy repeated, but it didn't sound as frightening when he did it.

'Try it lower,' said Aloysius.

Toddy had another shot: 'Nye-he-he-he-he.' It still wasn't frightening.

'Try it higher,' Aloysius suggested.

'Nye-he-he-he-he,' Toddy tweeted.

'Nah,' said Aloysius. 'S'not evil enough.'

'Evil,' said Toddy. 'It's not bad enough,' said Aloysius.

'Bad,' said Toddy.

'See if bagging the Chicken Bump makes you feel nastier,' Aloysius said.

Toddy smiled his bad-est smile. He advanced on Lorni, one threatening step at a time. To his surprise, Lorni advanced right back at him.

'What have you done with Dog?' Lorni asked menacingly. 'What have you done with all the Bumps inna OOB?'

'Put 'em inna juice machine,' said Toddy, 'an' squashed the Power out of 'em, yeah . . . 'cause we're bad! An' now we need some more juice, an' you look like a juicy chicken to me!'

'That's not nice,' Lorni replied, 'and you got it a-a-ll wrong.'

'Oh yeah?' said Toddy, and flicked out his claws.

'Yes,' said Lorni, calmly. 'I amn't the Chicken Bump. I'm the Curiosity Bump . . . and you know what Curiosity does to cats? C'mere, cat.'

Toddy couldn't believe it. Chicken liver Snoop was coming to get him . . . had got him . . . was holding him off the ground.

'All right,' said Aloysius. 'That's enough. Gimme the cat.'

'Oooh. Sorry,' said Lorni. 'Is this yours?' Lorni lifted the struggling Toddy high in the air, threw him at Aloysius, ran to the library door, waited for Aloysius and Toddy to sort themselves out and see where he'd gone, pulled a face at them, and ran off into the corridors with Toddy and Aloysius close behind.

Miz T and Sam floated through a bright and swirling world. There were cloud mountains, cloud valleys and then, in the distance, a cluster of Bumps all looking very busy. One was blowing on a gate, making it squeak with each puff. Another blew leaves in wild, swirling patterns. There were Bumps blowing clothes dry on clotheslines, Bumps making flags whip and crack in the wind of their out-breaths, Bumps flying kites by puffing up at them and . . . A big, round Bump floating from one group to another, watching and teaching them.

'What are they all doing?' Sam asked.

'Practising,' said Miz T. 'Air's a tricky element to handle. Hard to get a hold of. Your basic Air Bump is a balloon. Fills up with air and then lets it out to blow things. Very specialized. The one blowing the gate would never try leaves, and the one doing leaves never does kites. Like that. Takes lots of practice.'

The teacher noticed the newcomers, and floated quickly to them.

'Lutitia Tiggle,' he wheezed, 'as I live and breathe in and

blow out! It's been centuries. Welcome to the Air Academy and who's your little friend you're looking thin Lutitia both of you do try to remember to take in as much as you blow out as I'm always telling the younger Bumps being a balloon means air out *and* air in and . . .'

'Hot Air,' said Miz T, 'this is Sam. Sam, Hot Air. We're not balloons, dear. You are. What we are is in a hurry, and we need your help.'

'Oh, you're balloons all right,' Hot Air assured them. 'You have to take air in and send air out just like the rest of us. Same rules apply. You watch Robust Pickleswick over there, or the Breeze Brothers with those leaves, or Flapper blowing that flag or . . .'

''Scuse me,' Sam interrupted. 'Which one is Air?'

Hot Air was actually stopped, for a moment by Sam's question. Only for a moment, though. 'Air?' he said. 'As in *air*? The Air? The Big Ballooney?'

'Itself,' said Miz T. 'The Fourth Bump of the Aplopa-lypse,' Sam added.

Hot Air was amused. 'The Four Bumps of the Aplopa-lypse?' he laughed. 'No, no, no. That's just a myth . . . An ancient traditional story explaining things which cannot be explained, a story which is not true . . . all about balloons on pale horses with sharp tools I think . . . scythes and things . . . balloons can't stand sharp things you know. Ought to be a law. Is a law: Article 1234 of the pan-Galactic Whatsit which clearly says . . . hang on! Where are you going?'

As Hot Air rambled on, Miz T and Sam had been slipping quietly away.

'Love to stop and chat, my dear,' Miz T explained, 'but we are in a hurry . . .'

'And we do have to find the Air Bump,' Sam continued . . .

'And your class seems to be struggling with quite a strong wind over there,' Miz T added.

Hot Air saw that Miz T was right. The Balloon Bumps were being buffeted by a terrible wind, and it was getting stronger and suddenly Hot Air was shouting, 'It's the Ill Wind! It's the Ill Wind!' He ran toward his students, yelling out instructions. 'Let out your air!' he called. 'Tie your strings! It's the Ill Wind!'

As Sam and Miz Tiggle watched, a dark smudge on the horizon became a dark wind driving the Balloon Bumps before it. It was a wind with a face, a face with teeth, a face deserving the name Ill Wind. Riding on it, laughing wildly, was the Ink Thief. Behind him was Jim, feeding the Thief Power.

'Yeee haa!' the Thief whooped. He was having fun.

Jim wasn't. 'We're using more Power than I thought,' he complained. 'You said no one's seen the Air Bump since the start of the universe. They probably won't find it. I think we have to turn back. I think we have to turn back *now*!'

'Probably's not good enough,' the Thief replied. 'We have to be sure. Anyhow, this is *fun*. Have you no sense of fun, my boy? You have to use Power. That's what it's for. Hold on. I'm going to dive at them. Yeee ha!'

There was no place to hide as the Ill Wind hit the Air Bumps and scattered them.

Now we're high in the clouds. A bright yellow Balloon Bump is letting out its air and zooming around the sky like a drunken rocket. It blasts wildly through the clouds and . . . stay with it and watch as clouds spin crazily and the yellow balloon dives at the Ill Wind and . . . watch Jim's eyes widen as the Balloon comes straight at him and . . .

The Balloon smacked straight into Jim, knocking him off the Ill Wind. He tumbled through the sky, shouting 'HAAAAAAaaaaaallllp!!!!!!!!'

Sam saw him fall. 'Jim!' she screamed. 'Oh, Miz Tiggle. . . . Ji-i-i-mmm!!'

Sam could only watch in horror as her brother tumbled toward the ground with the yellow balloon spinning wildly around him. The Balloon crashed. Then Jim crashed . . . directly on top of it. The remaining air was knocked out of the balloon with a loud *Umpffffffffffff!!!* Jim rolled off it and stood up . . . unhurt.

'He's all right!' Sam cried. 'Come on, Miz Tiggle. He's all right! Jim!' Sam ran toward her brother. 'Jim!' she shouted. 'It's me. Sam! Oh, Jim!'

Jim saw his sister and Miz Tiggle running towards him. For a moment he hesitated, then . . . he turned and ran away from them.

'Jim!' Sam yelled.

'Stop! James Waverley, you get back here right *now*!'

As Sam and Miz Tiggle chased Jim across the cloudscape, a dark shadow fell over them. The Ill Wind carried the Thief to Jim . . . and Jim grabbed his outstretched hands . . . just as Sam grabbed Jim's feet.

'Sam!' Jim screeched. 'Let go! You're hurting me!'

Hearing that she was hurting Jim made Sam let go before she could think about it. It was only as Jim was lifted away that she realized what had happened and yelled at him: 'You're hurting yourself! I didn't have to let go of you. You could have let go of him!'

Almost all of the OOB are now smiling, snoring toys in the Toy Shop window. Only Dog and Lorni are missing to make a complete set. Now the toy merry-go-round begins to turn, starts to drop through the floor of the display and . . .

Dog sat alone and miserable in the cage, watching Jim and the Thief.

'It's very close,' Jim said. 'There might be just enough Power.'

He indicated the Ink Timer. It was almost empty. 'There isn't much time, though,' he continued. 'What actually happens if the timer runs out before you have enough Power to be Real?'

'I'd have to start again from Nothing,' said the Thief. 'We'd have lost everything. Goodbye perfect world.'

'Then we can't let it happen,' Jim said.

'That's the stuff,' the Thief replied. 'You turn the machine on. I'll go get the Dog Bump. Every little Bump helps.'

The Thief approached Dog's cage, and Dog cowered away and growled and the Thief opened the cage and reached for her and . . . The door of the lair was kicked off its hinges by . . . Lorni Snoop! He stomped into the lair and . . . Toddy and Aloysius rushed in behind him and grabbed his arms.

'Look boss,' Toddy chortled, 'we got another Bump!'

Lorni shrugged his shoulders . . . and Toddy and Aloysius were sent crashing together into a tangled heap on the ground! Without saying a word, Lorni advanced on the Thief with his new gunfighter style. The Thief's lips twitched. They slithered into a smile.

The Thief has left the cage open. Now Dog slips out. She edges along the wall, sees Lorni facing off with the Thief . . . and runs for all she's worth out of the lair as . . . the Thief puts his fingers in his pockets like guns, then draws them on Lorni, and they blaze with Power, and . . .

Lorni Snoop stands tall at the back of the display in the Toy Shop window, a huge silly grin on his face, snoring with all the other toyed Bumps.

*

Sam and Miz Tiggle wandered through clouds with the empty Balloon who knocked Jim down and then broke his fall.

'But you could have killed him,' Sam complained.

'But I saved him,' the Balloon replied. 'I wuz *angry*. They called up the Ill Wind. *Anything* might've happened. I mean where *is* everybody?'

Miz T moved faster. Sam and the Balloon had to hurry to keep up.

'Well, I, for one, am running out of patience,' Miz T said. 'We'd better get those bliddy pigglin' Bumps together bliddy pigglin' fast! I'm going to get that putherfuglin trundlefragit of an excuse for an Ink Thief, and I'm going to get my Bumps back, and *then* I'm going to . . .'

Dog sat in the shadows of the dark library, hoping Miz Tiggle would come back in time. She looked as sad as a Dog Bump can look, which is very. She sighed. She pulled herself together. She decided to go back for Lorni. She ran for the door. No. That was no good. She could never get him out. She decided to go find Miz Tiggle. She went to get the Strange Books. She stopped. No. Someone had to stay and be Watchdog. Look what happened last time she left. She tried to think of something. She couldn't. All she could do was howl a little blues. It was a sad, moonlight tune, finishing with a long, unhappy 'Harroooooooooooooooo'.

Dog was startled out of her skin by the sound of applause coming from the Strange Books across the room. The applause was followed by voices.

'Hey, you're not a bad singer.'

'Maybe you should give up being a dog and try show biz.'

''Course it isn't going to help that you look like a dog.'

Fascinated, Dog crept up to the Books, was startled again as one fell off the shelf and flopped open, and . . . Dog's eyes widened. She wagged her tail excitedly.

'Are you waving your bottom for exercise,' asked a voice, 'or are you just happy to see us?'

The pathetic looking, deflated Balloon sat on a cloud with Sam and Miz Tiggle. Sam and Miz T looked pretty deflated themselves.

'No Air Bump,' said Sam.

'Bumps,' said the Balloon.

'Bump,' said Miz T.

'Bumps,' said the Balloon.

'Bump,' said Sam.

'Bump,' said Miz T.

'Bumps,' said the Balloon. 'The plural of "Bump" is "Bumps". One Bump. Two Bumps. Lots of . . . Bumps. Only one . . . Bump. We're looking for lots and lots of Bumps.'

'No we're not,' Sam said.

'We're not?' asked the Balloon, surprised.

'We're looking for *the* Bump,' said Miz T. 'Singular. *The* Air Bump. The Big Ballooney. Only. Now we've got that cleared up, any ideas?'

'No,' said the Balloon, 'but I got a question. What are you lookin' for *ME* for?'

Jim lay asleep, sweating and looking as though he was having terrible dreams. The Thief, Aloysius and Toddy stood nearby, looking at the Ink Timer. It was almost empty. 'They may have found the Air Bump,' the Thief was saying. 'It's possible. Just a little more Power, my dears.

There will be a few stray Bumps around still. Gurgle Bumps in the plumbing. Banging Bumps in the roof. Perhaps a Squeak in a hinge. Find them my dears. We have to be sure we have enough Power to defeat the four Bumps and become Real ourselves. More than Real.'

Aloysius suddenly looked interested. 'Ourselves?' he asked.

'But surely you didn't think I'd become anything without you and dear Toddy,' said the Thief, 'did you? We're in this together, my dears. Now make preparations for one final Bump hunt. Do your worst. Excel yourselves. Drain the last few useless scraps of Imagination. Find the last few Things That will ever Go Bump. It's the Dusk of a new Night, my friends. Let's be ready for it.'

The Little Balloon, who had turned out to be the Big Ballooney, bounced heavily along with Miz Tiggle and Sam. Then, with a final splot, she stopped. 'This is the place,' she said. 'Drops straight out into the Spiral.'

The three of them sank slowly into the clouds. Miz Tiggle was not amused.

'Why,' she asked sternly, 'didn't you *tell* us you were the Big Ballooney?'

'You didn't ask,' the Balloon replied.

'But you're empty,' said Sam. 'There's nothing in you. You lost all your Air. Can you still be the Fourth Bump of the Aplopalypse?'

The Big Ballooney flexed her absence of muscles. 'Sweetie,' she said, 'I used to *work* to be like this before a tour. Let's go get the rest of the guys and I'll show you how it's done.'

*

The Ink Thief stands before an easel, putting the finishing touches on a portrait of Miz Tiggle. It looks like her, in a sour-pussed sort of way. Satisfied, he walks to a table covered in quill pens and . . . cocktail glasses? He drains something with fruit and a little umbrella in it and calls out: 'Toddy! Another pitcher of Power Sours and a bottle of Puissance Brute, I think.' Picking up one of the plumes on his desk, he turns and fires it like a dart into the portrait of Miz Tiggle.

Jim is deep in the Book of the Ink Thief. He pull his face out long enough to look worried, then does his disappearing head trick again, apparently sticking it into another dimension. When he returns his worry has turned to panic. He counts the Power containers on the shelf. It doesn't take long to count to three.

Aloysius had a mop in one hand, and a big sack in the other. Toddy watched as the Rat held up the mop, then the bag. 'Okay,' Aloysius said. 'Here's the Bump . . . and here's the bag. Show me what you're gonna do.' Toddy nodded. He took a deep breath. He attacked the mop. He bit it. He clawed it. He wrestled with it and . . . the mop slipped and hit him in the head. He attacked again, got a leg around the mop, pulled, and flipped himself over onto his back, tied in a knot. He couldn't move. Aloysius looked at the tangled, struggling mess on the ground, and sighed.

The Thief sipped a Power cocktail as he pulled a number of pen-darts out of Miz Tiggle's portrait. He returned the pens to the table, poured another drink, and tried to look interested as Jim rushed to him, babbling scientific words the Thief would never understand.

'It uses catalytic action,' Jim exclaimed, 'but with very unconventional catalytic agents, and they're going to get the right one, and it's going to work unless we stop them!'

'Fascinating, I'm sure,' the Thief lied. 'Jim, dear, I *am*

working. I have any amount of Power to get through, and then there are the eye and the reflexes to sharpen . . .'

So saying, the Thief lifted a pen and fired it at the Miz Tiggle target. He missed. 'There,' he said. 'You see what happens when I'm disturbed? It's not that I wouldn't like to chat with you about science, my dear, but . . .'

Suddenly, Jim seemed to change the subject. 'What kind of Bump is a Bootlig Bump Alley Cat?' he asked.

'How should I know?', the Thief replied. 'Who cares which kind of Bump is what? If you've seen one Bump, you've seen them all.'

'Miz Tiggle's plan will work because she knows about the catalyst,' Jim said. 'It's in the Strange Books. I looked. Whatever the Bootlig Bump Alley Cat is, if it gets near the Four Bumps nothing can stop them.'

Now the Thief was listening. 'I see,' he said. 'Any idea where one finds a . . . whatever you called it . . . cat?'

'The Strange Book says it's always found in the Wrong Place at the Wrong Time,' said Jim. 'I was hoping you'd know what that meant.'

'No, I don't,' said the Thief, leaning against his painting, 'but I know someone who should.' The Thief's shadow fell across the portrait of Miz Tiggle. He smiled.

CHAPTER SEVEN

Can This Really
Be The End?

Toddy stalks down a corridor, sack in hand, a picture of determination, and sees ... Messa Sloppit coming towards him. He doesn't hesitate. He prepares his bag and pounces. Messa too does not hesitate. She mops him. She hits him with six kinds of goo. She sloppifies him.

Miz Tiggle slapped open the parlour door and stamped in, followed by Sam and Dog. Dog was being comforted by Sam.

'Poor ol' Lorni,' Dog whined. 'Poor Lorni.'

'Don't worry,' Sam said. 'We're going to get him back. We're going to get them all back.'

Miz Tiggle looked more angry than worried as she went to the Strange Books. She chose one, and knocked on its spine. 'Right,' she said. 'Come on, you lot. It's show-time!'

Wafting from the book came four washes of colour ... four Bumps ... The Four Bumps of the Aplopalypse.

'Are you ready?' Miz T demanded.

'Are we *ready*?' said Rock. 'Hey. . . .'

Without another word, Rock pulled out his guitar and rocked. He was brilliant, as usual. Storm thundered out a bass line and did a lightning-show. Cheesey did a smell solo so strong it produced groans and holding of noses. Then the Big Ballooney took the stage. She stood. She wobbled. She plopped airlessly down to a floppy sitting position and . . . the other three Bumps went wild! They crowded around her.

'What can I say?' Rock said. 'You're better than ever. You're in good shape, girl.'

Miz Tiggle, Sam and Dog joined the happy Bumps. Miz T looked down at the small and pathetic Big Ballooney.

'In good shape, is she?' said Miz T.

'Better than ever,' said Rock. 'I wouldn't want to be that Ink Thief when *she* gets to him.'

'Why not?' asked Sam.

'Quite,' said Miz T. 'Well, the Strange Books say you Four can stop anybody. Are you ready to stop the Thief?'

'I'm ready to go on up and see him right now,' Cheesey offered.

'Well, then,' Miz T said, 'let's do it.'

'Right,' Storm agreed. 'Let's party. Where's the cat?'

'Cat?' Dog growled. 'What cat? Where's a cat!?!'

Miz T looked as though all the strength had drained out of her. 'Oh, dear,' she said. 'Uh. Ohh!!'

'What's wrong?' Sam asked.

Miz T pulled herself together. 'Frathersnaggits!' she said. 'The Catalyst! We forgot the Catalyst! The Bootlig Bump Alleycat. I must be losing my index cards. Sam and Dog come with me. You Four stay here, and stay ready.'

Rock shrugged, and picked up his guitar. 'No problem,' he said. 'We'll rehearse. We're the best, but who knows? We might even get *better*.'

Miz Tiggle, Sam and Dog were out the door and into the many doored corridor. Sam was puzzled and worried. 'You don't know where The Wrong Place at the Wrong Time *is*?' she asked angrily.

'Don't know when it is, either,' said Miz T as she marched along.

'Then why,' asked Sam, 'are we bothering? Where are we going? What . . .'

'The Catalyst is in a place,' said Miz T, 'right?'

'Right,' Sam agreed, 'but . . .'

'And it's there at a time, right?'

'Right, but how . . . ?' Sam asked.

'I know a short cut,' Miz T said.

'To where?' Sam asked.

'Everyplace,' Miz T said, '. . . *and* every time. There's not many Bump Cats. Usually one to the Universe, and Dog will smell it a galaxy away.'

'They *stinks*,' Dog spat.

'But we don't have *time* . . .' Sam began.

'Won't take time,' said Miz T. 'Least not much. We've got to go get it, y'know. The Four Bumps are about as useful as they look without that cat for a Catalyst. Right, the Universe starts . . . at that door and it finishes . . . at that one.'

'What,' Sam said, 'the whole Universe?'

'Every place,' Miz T assured her. 'Right or wrong, and every time likewise. Let's get that Catalyst.'

Miz Tiggle threw the door open. There was Nothing inside. 'You afraid?' she asked Sam.

'To jump?' Sam said. 'No. I'm just afraid we won't find the Catalyst in time.'

'Person who isn't afraid to jump into the Universe doesn't have to be afraid of anything,' said Miz T. 'Let's just go get that cat.'

They prepared to jump. 'Ready?' said Miz T. 'One . . .'

'Three!' said Dog. She started to jump. Then she remembered.

'No! Two!'

It was too late. 'OOOOOooooooooowwwwwwww . . .' she howled as she went.

'Come on,' Miz T said to Sam, and they jumped into emptiness, and . . .

The Ink Thief and Jim stepped out of hiding and watched them go.

'You see?' the Thief said. 'Simple. Just follow those idiots!'

The Thief and Jim left the door open when they jumped after Sam and Miz T. It was Messa Sloppit who closed it. She just happened to be mucking and yucking her way up the corridor. She saw the open door, looked through at the Universe . . . and was revolted.

'The Universe,' she slobbered. 'Uck!'

She slammed the door shut and rolled her cart away, mumbling disgustedly.

While the other three practise for their showdown with the Ink Thief, the Big Ballooney wobbles out into the library. She walks down a row of books, looking with interest at all the titles. What she doesn't notice, but we do (if we're sharp), is a pair of raggedy feet on the window sill. It's Toddy. He stands absolutely still, like a gargoyle, and the Big Ballooney walks right under him and . . . Toddy pounces. He bangs her. He bites her. He wrestles her limbs into knots and . . . Ballooney loves it. She thinks they're dancing. Toddy is desperately puzzled . . . then it dawns on him. I catched a Bump. I catched a Bump! I *catched a Bump!! BAD CAT!!! AAaaow!!!!*

When Toddy showed up with his Bump, the Boss was out. Aloysius was home though, and he was impressed. 'I never thought you'd do it, cat,' he said. 'Kinda small and crummy looking . . . but it's a Bump all right.'

Ballooney just stood there looking pathetic, helpless, and perfectly happy. 'It was a tough one,' Toddy boasted, 'but I was tougher. It was a rough one . . . but I was . . . stinkier. I had killery stinks! I grobalized it, *and* then I bonged it, and then it cotched me, but I leapeded back, just like you showed me, elbows out, claws out, and then I . . .'

'Cat,' Aloysius said, 'go turn on the machine and put the monster in it before it dies of old age.'

'The monster' looked as harmless as a baby. Toddy approached her carefully, looking bad. He showed his claws . . . and the BB smiled.

'See that Power Machine over there?' Toddy growled. 'Well, that's where you're going. Inside it. An' we're gonna squish all your Power out.' The Air Bump smiled again. 'Okay,' she said, and walked toward the machine. Toddy had to think about this, but the was soon in charge of the situation again. He got behind Ballooney and herded her threateningly in the direction she was already going.

'Don't try to run,' he said. 'Don't try to fight. Other end, over there, where the steps are. That's it. Better not mess with me, 'cause Toddy's a *bad* cat.'

The door to the Universe burst open and Dog came flying out, sniffing and speaking at lightning speed. 'No cat,' she sniffed – 'No cat – sniff – no cat – sniff – no cat – sniff – no . . . oh!'

Miz Tiggle and Sam joined Dog. They didn't look too happy about the Universe or Anything.

'There has to be a Bootlig Bump Alley Cat,' Miz T was saying. 'There *has* to be!'

'But there isn't,' said Sam. 'Dog sniffed the whole Universe.'

Dog's head inserted itself sharply between Miz Tiggle's

and Sam's. She sniffed. 'Yes?' she barked. 'Sniff – sniff – sniff . . . *Yes?* – sniff – sniff – sniff . . . *YES!*'

'When you say yes . . .' said Miz T.

'You mean . . .?' said Sam.

'YES, CAT!' Dog howled. 'Bump Cat. Here! Now!'

'Funny,' Miz T said. 'I'd have thought here and now was the Right place and the Right time to find it, not the Wrong Place and the Wrong Time.'

'Well, where is it?' Sam asked, impatiently.

'Where's what?' said Dog.

'The *Bump Cat*!'

'Oh,' said Dog. 'Yeah.' Dog began to sniff again, and they all followed her nose down the corridor as . . .

A triumphant looking Thief and a frazzled Jim emerged out of the Universal door.

'It's all over,' the Thief exclaimed. 'They found no cat, so there will be no Four Bumps of the Aplopalypse. Today's the day, Jim. We use all the Power we have. Today I become Real. Today I become Somebody, and we start on that perfect world, my boy.'

'And I go home,' said Jim. 'With Sam.'

'Yes, Jim,' the Thief assured him. 'You'll have served your . . . done your job, and I'm sure I'd enjoy taking your sister away from Tiggle. Yes, Jim, today's the day.'

The Big Ballooney sits in the hopper of the Power Machine, looking pretty excited about the whole thing. 'Hey, turn on the ride,' she shouts.

Aloysius looks at Toddy. 'Weird,' he says.

Toddy is determined. He strides over to the Machine. 'There's no use beggin' for mercy,' he says, 'and there's no use tryin' to trick me. When I catch 'em, they stay catched . . . and I *squish* out the Power.'

Toddy flips on the first switch, and the Machine begins to turn, and he operates the wheels and levers and the Machine steams and Ballooney, even more excited now that the 'ride' is finally going, chortles a little ditty to herself and disappears into the workings of the Machine. It grinds and bubbles away as usual, processing her.

Toddy watched the Machine with pride. Aloysius took a bottle of Power off the shelf behind him. He pulled it open with his teeth. 'It's a big moment, cat,' he said. 'Yer first Bump. Let's drink to it.'

'Oh, no,' wailed Toddy, 'we couldn't. Oh no, we shouldn't. There's only . . . 1, 3, 9 . . . elevendy six bottles left. What would the Boss say?'

'He's never gonna know, is he?' said Aloysius.

'He isn't?'

'Nah cat, 'cause we're gonna use the Power from the Bump you caught to fill it up again, right?' Aloysius explained.

'Oohh,' said Toddy. 'Riiight.'

They drank. Their eyes widened. They glowed. They held themselves more erect. 'Ahh,' Aloysius sighed. 'That's the stuff. I feel nastier already. When I'm a real person I'm gonna be a real rat.'

'Me too,' said Toddy. 'I'm gonna be a person with killery stinks. I'm gonna be the badest.'

'Right,' Aloysius said. 'Let's go get the Power from yer Bump. Maybe there's enough to fill the bottle and have another little drink for ourselves.'

'Nice,' purred Toddy.

They stood at the Power outlet. There was nothing. The bucket below it was empty.

'Nothin'?' said Aloysius.

'Couldn't be nothin',' Toddy said. 'I put the Bump in. I runned the Machine. *Has* to be Power in the bucket. Has to be Power to put back in the bottle, 'cause when the boss comes back . . . go 'way. I'm thinkin' . . . 'Cause when the boss comes back . . .'

Toddy stopped . . . realized that someone was pulling on his sleeve . . . counted Aloysius, then himself, then . . . looked slowly around and saw . . . the Big Ballooney!

'That was fun,' she giggled. 'Les do it again.'

Sam and Miz T followed Dog's nose to a door. They eased it open and peeked through into . . . the Ink Thief's lair! There were Aloysius and Toddy, fussing manically with the Power Machine. Miz Tiggle's eyes lit up and she was a bit manic herself as she whispered: 'That's it! That's him! It's he! *That's* the . . .' Miz T began . . .

'Bump Cat!' barked Dog.

'Of course!' Miz T said. 'He's the Catalyst. It was all that stuff in the Strange Book about being in the wrong Place at the Wrong Time that fooled me. It's not the wrong time and place for *US* he has to be in . . . It's the wrong time and place for *HIM* . . . and I think I know how to get him there. Let's . . .'

Dog grabbed Miz T and sniffed in the direction of the door. 'Smells like Ink Thief comin' . . . sounds like Ink Thief comin' . . .'

'Then let's go before he sees us,' Miz T said. 'I have a plan.'

'Oh, good,' said Sam. 'Another plan.'

Toddy and Aloysius are frantic. They run to the Power Bucket. No Power. They run back to the other end of the Machine, open the hopper, and the Big Ballooney's head pops up. 'This is great,' she squeals. 'Run it again. I'm ready.'

Cat and Rat look at each other with confusion which becomes panic as they hear the sweet voice of their Master calling: 'Toddy! Aloysius! The hour is upon us!'

The Thief and Jim walked into the lair.

'The time has come,' the Thief said. 'A new night is falling, and I will drink until . . . Ah!' The Thief saw the opened, empty Power bottle. He saw the empty space where it should have been on the shelf. He picked the bottle up and turned it over. Not a drop trickled out. Jim was horrified. The Thief just sighed. He even managed a smile as Toddy and Aloysius came shuffling along in answer to his call.

'That shelf is all the Power that's left,' Jim said. 'How *could* you?'

'I'm sure they can explain,' the Thief said. 'Toddy? Aloysius?'

'I'm ashamed, yer Awfulness,' the Rat rumbled.

'Well, you should be,' Jim said.

'Well, I am. I shoulda stopped him.'

'Me, too,' said Toddy.

'Whod'a thought,' said Aloysius, 'that the ol' cat would steal from you like that.'

'Yeah,' said Toddy, 'whod'a thought . . . huh?'

'I don't want to hear another word,' the Thief said. 'Toddy, go find a Bump to fill this bottle, and don't come back without one. Aloysius —'

Toddy, not much of a thinker at the best of times, was too upset to think at all. Before he knew what he was doing, he'd grabbed the Boss's coat to get his attention and explain. He looked at his hands. He realized what he'd done. 'Yeee*EE*!' he said, as he pulled his hand away and then: 'But I *got* a Bump. Bottle's *empty* 'cause I caught a

Bump . . . only I couldn't fill the bottle 'cause the Bump's empty too, so I had an empty bottle and an empty Bump. See, there it . . . Aloysius, where's a Bump gone?'

There was, of course, no sign of the Big Ballooney.

'What Bump?' asked Aloysius, innocently.

'Aloysius,' the Thief said quietly, 'please find Toddy a Bump bag and show him how to use the door. Jim, dear, come with me.'

As Jim followed the Thief to his desk, Aloysius led a stunned Toddy to a bag, then to the door.

'I'm a rat,' the Rat explained. 'I had to blame you. Hey, it's not easy bein' a rat. Go get that Bump . . . and bring home a full one this time.' Aloysius threw the confused and dejected cat out into the corridor. Then he smiled his nasty, toothy smile. 'It's not easy bein' a rat,' he repeated to himself. 'HEH-heh-heh-heh-heh.'

Toddy stands miserably in the corridor. Why go on? Why bother? Nobody wants him. Nobody loves him. Nobody even likes him. All he ever wanted out of life was . . . a fish? Toddy blinks in disbelief and looks again at the ground in front of him. Looks like a fish. Smells like a fish. Toddy creeps slowly toward the large fish on the corridor floor and . . . the fish, just as slowly, begins to slide down the corridor. Toddy moves faster. So does the fish. He slows down. The fish does likewise. Toddy stops . . . then rushes for the fish which whips away and is followed by Toddy around a corner and out of sight.

Jim was a bundle of frayed nerves as he moved around the desk and apparatus. The Thief relaxed with a pot of Power, sipping it and practising trick shots with the quill pens. The pens left his hand from all sorts of flash positions, and hit their target with a satisfying 'thwack'.

'I don't know,' Jim fussed. 'I don't know. I just don't *know*. I think there's enough Power to make you Real, but then what? We'll need more to get Sam back, and Miz Tiggle will still try to stop you, and we need Power to start making the world a better place because otherwise what's the point of it all, and the Ink Timer's almost empty so we have to move fast, but we can't move fast on *everything* because we don't have enough Power, so the question is . . .'

'Jim, dear boy,' the Thief interrupted, 'you *must* stop fussing. A Man doesn't fuss. Bumps and women fuss. A Man uses strategy, tactics, science. So. You've listed the problems. Now, without emotion, let's think . . . while I drink.'

Jim tried to think. He tried to be scientific. He tried not to panic. The Thief sipped his cup of Power, and was very quiet. Then his lips twitched, and the serpent of his smile snaked across his face. 'Mmm . . .' he said. 'I see a way. Oh, yes. That's elegant. Terribly, terribly elegant. So many problems solved at once. Jim! Take a letter.'

Jim prepared the quills and ink, and the Ink Thief began. 'Dear Sam,' he dictated . . . and Jim stopped writing.

'No,' Jim said. 'Keep Sam out of this. She's . . .'

'I'm trying', said the Thief, 'to *get* her out of it, my dear. I want to get you back together and send you home. That's the most important thing, isn't it? Whether my plans succeed or not, there must be a happy ending for you. No, don't thank me. Just write. "Dear Sam, I've found a way out of here. Come right away. Don't tell anyone what you're doing. Don't let anyone see you. Go out into the corridor and" . . .'

*

Sam, Dog and the Four Bumps peeked out of the parlour door into the corridors.

'I gotta tell ya, Ballooney,' Rock whispered, 'ya had us worried.'

'You sure you're all right?' Cheesey asked.

'Oh, yeah,' the tiny Big Ballooney bubbled. 'It was really nice. I got to go on a great ride an' everything.'

'Shhhh!' Sam said. 'Here they come.'

Over Sam's shoulder we can see Miz Tiggle walking slowly backwards through the door and into the parlour. As she comes we see that she's handling a fishing line, pulling it carefully. Once she's inside the parlour, Miz T motions to everyone to be quiet. She pulls the fishing line gently, then gives a final, *big* tug and . . . a fish flies in through the door, followed by a flying Toddy. He leaps on the fish. He holds it triumphantly, inhales its wonderful perfume, is about to take that first, mind-blowing lick and . . . he stops. He realizes that he's not in the corridor any more. He's in a room. He's not alone. He is, in fact, surrounded.

Ballooney was delighted to see Toddy in the parlour. 'Hey,' she said, 'it's him! It's the cat that does the rides. Hiya, pussycat!'

Toddy backed away from the Big Ballooney. 'It wasn't me,' he growled, '. . . an' it's *my* fish . . . an' . . . don' call me a puzzycat . . . an' . . .'

Backing away from the others sent Toddy directly into . . . Dog. He turned slowly. He saw her. He said, '*EEEEeee!!!*'

'*AAHHhhrrrr!!!!!!*' Dog replied, and attacked.

She batted the fish from his hand, started to bang him around and . . . Miz Tiggle stepped in. She held Dog in one hand, and Toddy in the other.

'Now, Dog,' she said, 'Toddy's going to be our friend, remember? Give him back his fish.'

Miz T let go of Dog. Dog gave Toddy back his fish.

Well, actually she smacked him in the face with it, but at least he got it back.

'Would you like some milk?' Miz T asked.

'Uh . . .' said Toddy, 'yeah.'

Miz T patted Toddy's head. 'And then a little nap?' she asked.

'Mmmmm. Yeah,' Toddy purred.

Aloysius looked at the Thief with admiration. 'So we're gonna kidnap the girlie,' he said. 'Fun, fun, fun. Whada life.'

'Not kidnap,' the Thief corrected, 'save . . . from the awful Tiggle. She's not going to be a hostage, she's going to be our guest . . . unless Tiggle should want to try anything . . . like getting her back, or stopping us, or using the Four Bumps, or irritating me even in the slightest way.'

Jim looked tired almost beyond hope as the Ink Thief went to him. The Thief stroked his hair, and spoke gently. 'Come,' he said. 'It's time you got your sister back.' Jim looked up, and a spark of brightness returned at the mention of his Sam.

Toddy was in heaven. Sam and Cheesey were feeding him goodies. Rock dangled bits of his foliage for him to play with. Storm cooled him with breezes, and the Big Ballooney snuggled up with her new friend while Miz T rubbed his tummy. Dog watched from the other side of the parlour. 'Disgustin'!' she grumbled to herself. ''Orrible stupid cat. Any pettin' goes on around here's supposed to be for *ME*.'

The Thief, Aloysius and Jim lurk outside the door to the parlour. The Thief pulls out a vial of Power and downs it, and Jim whispers worriedly: 'You *can't* use more Power. You need every drop we've got.'

'I have to, my boy,' the Thief replies, 'for you.'

Watch the Thief's hands as he does a complex series of gestures and calls up a grey swirl of energy. He takes out Jim's note to Sam, shows it to Jim, then throws it into the swirling greyness. Jim watches as the note fades away.

No one noticed the smudge of greyness swirling through the parlour door. No one saw Jim's note drop lightly into Sam's hand. No one, that is, except Sam. She looked, saw the handwriting on the note, and gasped. Quietly, without anyone seeing, she read it. Equally quietly, she stood up. The others were busy preparing Toddy to be the Catalyst for the Four Bumps. As Sam nonchalantly walked by them, they were working hard on Toddy.

'What a brave cat,' Miz T said, patting him.

'Yeah,' said Toddy the Hero, 'an' the Four Bumps don't haveta be afraid, 'cause I'll be the Catalyst . . . *and* brave!'

Sam slips through the parlour door into the corridor. She walks off into the dusty dimness and . . . an awful hand reaches out from hiding and covers her mouth. More hands, none of them pleasant looking, pull her out of sight.

Toddy and the Four Bumps were ready to rock 'n' roll. The Ink Thief had been cruel to Toddy, and now he'd be sorry. Dog watched Toddy playing hero with increasing disgust.

'Follow me, fellas!' Toddy called, and started for the door.

'No, no, no, no, no, no, no,' Ballooney interrupted. 'That's not how it works. *We* have to go in first, *then* the Catalyst.'

'Big Ballooney's right,' Cheesey agreed. 'Gotta put the elements in before the Catalyst.'

'And follow them with the very best Catalyst there is,' said Miz T, making sure Toddy stayed with them.

'That's *me*!' said Toddy.

'Right,' said Miz T.

'Right,' said Toddy. 'Goofer it, guys. I'm right behind ya.'

'Goofer it?' Rock asked, then shrugged and headed off to do what an Aplopalyptic Bump's gotta do. With Storm thundering and zapping behind him, Rock threw open the door and the Four Bumps of the Aplopalypse blazed off down the corridor to finish with the Ink Thief. Miz T was left in silence with Dog and Toddy.

'Where's Sam?' she asked. 'It's almost time. Frathersnaggits, where *is* that girl? You two stay here. I'll go find her.'

Miz Tiggle hurried off to the library. Toddy practised being an important hero. Dog watched with dark emotion. Finally she could stand it no more. 'Stupid cat,' she said. 'Smelly, stupid cat. Ugly, smelly, stupid . . .'

Toddy the hero was insulted. He went up to Dog. He removed one of his disgusting, fingerless gloves and . . . slapped Dog across the face with it. Dog sighed. Dog thought about what might be the best thing to do in such a situation. Dog grabbed hold of Toddy and thumped him and shook him and threw him around and chased him around the room, all the while discussing the situation with him.

'This isn't a Cat Bump place,' she snarled, '. . . this is a Dog Bump place . . . for Dog Bumps . . . and that's me and they was pettin' you and they wasn't pettin' me so bad cat! Go! . . . My place! . . . Go home! Go!'

Toddy got the message. He couldn't get out the door fast enough.

Toddy slumps down the corridor, trying doors at random. One opens. He looks in. It's Messa Sloppit's store cupboard. There's her trolley, mops and buckets of goo. There's gunge and streamers of yuck hanging from the walls and ceiling. It looks just the place. Toddy sits down with a sigh in the middle of the ickiness and his head drops into his hands.

Sam shouted and kicked as the Ink Thief dragged her down the dusty corridor. He had her arm twisted up behind her back. Aloysius followed them, with Jim.

'Jim!' Sam screamed at him. 'What's the matter with you? Make him let me go!'

Jim, torn and miserable, tried to think of something to say. He couldn't. Jim didn't do anything to stop him, but stop the Thief did. He smiled a slow smile. 'Aloysius,' he said, 'go. Warm up the Power Machine. I've just thought of something wonderful to put in it.'

'Yeah?' said Aloysius, having no idea what the Thief was talking about and . . . Aloysius looked at the Thief holding Sam, then at Sam and . . . 'Oh,' he said. 'Yyeah . . . nye he he he he he!'

As Aloysius went off down the corridor, the Thief turned his attention back to Sam. He twisted her arm until she had no choice but to follow him. Sam cried out from the pain, looked daggers at her brother, and was dragged away. Now even Jim began to understand. The confusion on his face giving way to horror and anger, and he followed the Thief . . . slowly at first . . . then faster and . . .

'Good thing you found it,' Miz T said as she studied Jim's note to Sam. 'Good Dog. Now where's the cat?'

'Oh, Miz Tiggle,' Dog howled, '. . . bad Dog! I chased cat and . . . and . . . it ran away. Thief's got Sam and no cat. Bad, bad, bad, bad Dog.'

'Well,' Miz T said, 'so much for things workin' out

by themselves. It's finally come down to it. Me against him.'

'Dog,' said Dog, 'against Cat.'

'Come on,' Miz T said. She hitched up her sleeves. Dog hitched up her fur. She hitched up her dress. Dog hitched up her other fur. They turned, and together they leapt through the wall in a blaze of energy.

Aloysius scuttles down the corridor. He stops. He sniffs. 'Cheese?' he says. 'A lot of cheese. A great lot of great cheese!' Aloysius sniffs his way to a door. He opens it. There, in all her smelly glory, is Cheesey. She floats in emptiness. Aloysius, he drools, and he runs toward her. As he comes Cheesey seems to drop away into the depths of the emptiness inside the door. Aloysius dives after her. As he shrinks to a dot, his screams sound as though he were falling a very, very long way.

The Thief pulled hard on Sam's arm, and she banged against the corridor wall. Jim was coming fast, and now his eyes widened. He could stand no more. He threw himself on the Thief.

'No!' he shouted. 'Stop! Let . . .' The Thief flicked Jim off and he hit his head. Hard. He felt it, saw the blood on his hands, got back to his feet. This time he threw himself as hard as he could, and the Thief lost his grip on Sam. She twisted away and ran, with Jim right behind her. The Thief laughed. He raised his hands and prepared to Power them to the floor and . . . Rock stepped into the passage in front of him.

'Come on,' he smiled. 'Let's get it on!'

The Thief blasted Power from both hands but . . . it was

too late. Rock expanded faster than the Thief's eyes could follow and . . . *WHUMP!* He was a stone wall, sealing off the corridor completely. No amount of Power blasting from the Ink Thief could even begin to move him. Snarling and white-lipped, the Thief turned and stalked away.

On the far side of Rock's wall, Jim held on to Sam and cried. 'Oh, Sam,' he moaned, 'I'm so stupid. I wanted to make things right with Power, but Power doesn't make things right. It doesn't matter how much Power you have. It's what you do with it.'

Sam's smile was wet with both their tears. 'You don't sound stupid to me,' she said. 'You sound different. You sound good. I missed you, Jim.'

'I missed you too,' Jim sniffed. 'I didn't know how much I missed you.'

'Had a bad moment of missing you myself,' said Miz T's voice.

'Me too,' said Dog.

Sam and Jim looked up. There were Miz Tiggle and Dog looking down at them.

'I'm very glad to see you two safe and together,' Miz T said. 'Don't know how you got that way, but we can talk later. Take care of 'em Dog. I've got to see a Bump about his behaviour.'

Before anyone could say a word, Miz Tiggle had pushed up her sleeves, hitched up her skirt and marched off. Sam watched her go. 'We better go after her,' she said. 'We got her into this. Come on. Dog will take care of us, right Dog?'

'Yeah!' said Dog. 'Right!' And the three of them followed Miz Tiggle, with Watchdog watching for danger on all sides.

*

The Thief takes the last containers of Power down from the shelf. He glances at the Ink Timer. It's dripping its last few drops. As he guzzles Power he hears a sound and . . . the Thief begins to feel . . . that there's someone . . . watching him. Down at the far end of the lair, in the dimness? Still swilling he goes to see and . . . lightning flares. Blinded, the Thief rushes back to his Power. He pours it down, then cries out to his unseen visitors: 'I'm ready. I'm full of Power. I'm making the Change. I'm becoming . . .'

The lightning flashes once more and, when the Thief can see again, there are Storm and the Big Ballooney. The Thief laughs at the sight of them, laughter which becomes increasingly mad as Miz Tiggle follows the two Bumps out of the dimness. As Storm flashes and thunders, Miz T folds her arms and glares at him. The Thief giggles wildly.

'I've protected you for a very long time,' Miz T said, 'but now it has to stop. Give the Power back to the Bumps and come home to the library.'

'Never!' the Thief shouted. 'I'm practically real, and you're not, so you can't be my sister, can you? You're not my sister, do you hear? You're not, and I'll have your Power too . . .'

The Thief lurched toward Miz Tiggle, who stood her ground. The Big Ballooney wasn't standing, though. She was moving forward. She slumped pathetically at the Thief. He watched her coming and . . . he laughed insanely and . . . he fired a stream of Power into the BB who . . . absorbed it! She began to inflate with the Power and she kept coming and the Thief kept firing, letting out all his Power in great blazing waves, and the empty little Big Ballooney became *big* as she took the Power in. She was almost bursting, straining at the seams when . . .

Toddy slipped through the door into the lair. This was in fact the Wrong Place and the Wrong Time for poor old

Toddy to come back, so the Strange Books were right about that. Toddy had forgotten about being the Catalyst, though. He was rehearsing. 'An' I'm gonna say Boss,' he said to himself . . . 'I'm sorry an' I'm back ta stay. I'm gonna be a bad cat, and you're gonna be proud of me, an' . . . uh-oh.'

Toddy saw what was happening to the Boss. 'Leave him alone, you bully!' he screamed, and ran to protect his Master just as . . . the Thief took all his remaining Power and fired a tremendous burst which . . . *caught Toddy* as he leapt between the Thief and the Big Ballooney. All that was left of Toddy was a smoking pair of shoes. The Ballooney was about to explode from holding all the Ink Thief's Power. 'Whew!' she said, 'it's a good thing the Catalyst got that last bit. I'd have burst if I'd took another drop.'

With no Power left, the Thief looked down at his body. 'I'm fading!' he cried.

Now it was Storm's turn to smile. She thundered. She flashed and . . . she bucketed rain down on the Thief and he tried to fight, and he tried to run, but without any Power he could only struggle blindly around the lair in Storm's driving rain. He crawled to the door. There in the doorway, watching, were Sam, Jim and Dog. Looking up at Jim, the Thief smiled through his tears. 'You'll want me back, my dear,' he whispered, 'and you'll call me . . . and I'll come to you.'

Sam and Jim backed away as the Thief dissolved into liquid, coloured, rapidly fading inks.

'Oh, Jim, he won't come back, will he?' Sam asked.

'Not if we don't want him to,' Jim said. 'It's our imagination.'

'Yours indeed,' Miz T said, coming up behind them. 'Everything is. You're the Owner of it all: Bumps, Library, Universe, and Toy Shop. The Owner's come back, the Ink

Thief's lease is up, and now it's time to go home. I'm going to miss you, Sam. I'm ... you're ... it's ... Most fun I've had since ... well ... that's another story. The way out's next to the Toy Shop window. Go out this door and turn—'

'The Toy Shop window!' Jim cried. 'The Bumps! I've got to run the Power Machine backwards!'

Running to the Machine, Jim pulled a big lever right over and uncoiled a hose. Sam ran to help, and they dragged the hose to the merry-go-round. It clipped in neatly. Holding the other end, Jim went up to the now Very Big Ballooney. 'We have to give all that Power back to the Bumps,' he said.

The Ballooney looked down at her hugely over-inflated body. 'Oh, thank goodness,' she said. 'If I had to get rid of it myself I'd be shooting around his place for centuries.'

Jim attached the hose and the Ballooney released all the Power into it. As she got smaller again, the Power poured through the hose, up the merry-go-round and ...

An incredibly silly Toy Shop window full of grinning and snoring Bumps became *phenomenally* silly as they all came back to life and found themselves jumbled together with their memories returning slowly. Before they had completely worked out who they were, or where, or why, Sam and Jim had joined them. Miz T and Dog appeared through a wall, followed by Storm and the Big Ballooney. Miz T showed Jim and Sam the way out through a little side door. Lorni ran and hugged Sam and Sam hugged all the Bumps and she hugged Dog and she hugged Jim and Dog hugged Jim and all the Bumps hugged Jim and Jim hugged all the Bumps and the high spirited, if still dopey Bumps all hugged each other, and Cheesey and Rock materialized and the Four Bumps looked mighty pleased with themselves and each other and ... Sam hugged Miz

Tiggle. They looked at each other for a long time, and then Miz T put an arm around Sam and one around Jim. 'Hurry home,' she said.

Sam just stood there, looking at Miz T and all the babbling Bumps. Finally, Jim took her hand. 'It's been such a long time,' he said. 'Mum and Dad must be frantic.'

'It's the evening of the very same day you came in here,' said Miz T. 'No one will be worried. No one will be upset. Off you go.' Sam lingered over letting go of Miz T. Then smiling, her eyes bright with tears, she turned and followed Jim out the little side door.

Miz T watched calmly as Sam left. Then she turned to the assembled Bumps.

'Yes,' she said. 'Well,' she said. 'That's that, then. Come on. Time for us all to go home.' The Bumps all thought home sounded good. It was only when they were all burbling in the general direction of the door that Miz T went to the boarded-up Toy Shop window. She pulled the loose board aside, and was just in time to see Sam and Jim walking off into the late summer sunset. She waved. They couldn't see her, of course, but she waved anyhow and fought back the tears.

Dog galloped toward Miz T, just as she turned away from the window. Sad face! Dog did her silliest smile. It didn't help. In fact, now that Dog thought about it, she was sad too. The two of them looked at each other for a long moment. Then . . . Dog pushed up her fur. Miz T smiled a little smile, and pushed up her sleeves. Dog hitched up her other fur. Miz T hitched up her dress and . . . Dog and librarian leapt through the wall and out of the Toy Shop.

EPILOGUE

In a world of smoke and mirrors, Toddy found that he was not alone. 'Oh, hiya Boss,' he said.

'Ah,' said the Ink Thief, 'Toddy.'

'I thought we was finished,' Aloysius said.

The Thief only smiled.

'Where've we gone, Boss?' Toddy asked.

'No place,' said the Thief. 'We're still right here, in the Imagination.'

'Well, what,' Toddy wondered, 'happens now?'

The Ink Thief laughed. 'We try again,' he said, 'only this time . . . Mmm hm-hm-hm . . . it's too good.' Still laughing, the Thief began to change, to morph, to melt into another shape. Only his laughter stayed the same.